I0783815

Of

Indomitable

Desire

Nik

Copyright © 2024 by Nik

All rights reserved.

No part of this publication may be reproduced, distributed, or transmitted in any form or by any means, including photocopying, recording, or other electronic or mechanical methods, without the prior written permission of the publisher, except as permitted by U.S. copyright law.

The story, all names, characters, and incidents portrayed in this production are fictitious. No identification with actual persons (living or deceased), places, buildings, and products is intended or should be inferred.

No part of this book may be used or reproduced in any manner for the purpose of training artificial intelligence technologies or systems.

Book Cover by Nik.

1st edition, 2024.

© Kirimizi

Dedicated to those who read too many books, play too many video games, and live in a world no one else can see.

I

"For the context of everyone here, please state your name and background."

"Is background necessary?" A low voice grumbled in response.

"The meeting must start as it always has, for hundreds of years before your time, and likely long after. Please state your name and background."

An elongated sigh left the lips of Islix, whose naturally large stature frightened those seated across from him. He had even done his long black hair back in a low bun in the way of his other soldiers in hopes of being less intimidating, but watching the reaction of the enemy army flinch as he rose from his seat, he realized quickly that it did nothing of effect for him. Unfortunately, placing his hair back prominently displayed his protruding charcoal horns sticking out of his faded crimson complexion. He blinked away his full black eyes from the army and looked to his own with a shrug.

In the barely lit meeting room sat a single cherry wood table, circular on opposing sides, but long in length. Surrounding the two armies were stone walls, bearing short cracks allowing in rifts of cold wind. The Royan castle didn't look too bad when he first approached with his army after being called in for a possible allyship, but the more of these meetings Islix attended, the more he noticed small things here and there; cracks in the structure, the fear in the eyes of the Royan army, the stress on the opposing generals older face, wrinkled with nothing but frustration.

He should have known something was wrong when the kingdom neighboring his own, known for their impulsive violence and their inability to assimilate to the newer world, had asked to discuss a possible alliance with the Indomnis people.

Islix stood in the middle of this table, facing the man who once threatened to eliminate his people, who threw slurs at him whenever they crossed paths, even swore to extinguish his bloodline. It never seemed possible to be asked for help from the same man.

And yet, here they were.

"My name is Islix of the Indomnis, or as you once called us, 'The Devil Clan', invited to the castle of the Royan people for talks of alliance. How was that?" Islix asked, smiling to himself for the added comment.

Beside him stood his second in command and best friend Aslin, whose own horns were short, sharp, and hidden by their short, clipped back black curls. Their lighter red skin tone settled brightly against her pitch black eyes, attentive and ready for anything. They nudged him in encouragement, along with a few scattered chuckles from remaining Indomnis soldiers on both sides of him.

The general across from him cleared his throat, gaining the attention of both groups.

"My name is Ozburn of the Royan, opening our doors for the Indomnis to talk of settling our differences." The older man struggled to say, his wrinkled pale complexion partly blushed as he fidgeted with his white mustache, but staring down at the other leader with his bold cerulean eyes.

"Anything else we need to do before beginning these discussions?" Islix asked, meeting Ozburn's intense gaze with his own.

"No." He said simply, sitting down in his chair, his soldiers following suit with the collective clatter of armor settling with them.

"Fine then." Islix nodded, gesturing for his own group of soldiers to sit before he did so himself, crossing one armored leg over the other. "Let us begin."

General Ozburn settled into his seat, clearing his throat before he began. "First order of business to begin these discussions, I would like to clarify what an alliance would do for the two kingdoms. Such an allyship would set in stone the union of the Royan and Indomnis people, meaning the two sides share resources with one another."

"Resources? Such as?" Islix repeated, suspicion rising in his thoughts.

"Well, I am sure you are aware that part of the land beneath the Indomnis had once belonged to the Royan kingdom. In our eyes, those metal deposits belong to us, but are simply within the name of another."

"Do you speak of the land that the Royan kingdom stole from the Indomnis over three hundred years ago that was reclaimed during the last war, also instigated by your side?" Islix asked, not allowing a single shift in his voice, lest it show some sign of weakness.

"Bygones, of course." General Ozburn waved his hand, refusing to acknowledge the details of the last war between the Indomnis and Royan kingdoms a mere one hundred years prior. "But in the spirit of peace, the sharing of resources would be beneficial for both sides."

"Elaborate." He straightened his back, awaiting to hear his explanation.

"When our armies combine into one, we will need to support one another, strength in numbers, as they say. But those numbers will require weaponry, and the resources you lay claim to would allow such a feature."

Islix looked to the stretch of Royan military across from him, eyeing the shiny armor and spotless scabbards attached to many of them.

"So, you ask for access, not only to our metal deposits, but our military as well?" Islix asked, unable to tear his eyes from the spotless sets on the soldiers seated across the table.

"In the spirit of alliance, yes. To help one another would be our ultimate goal." General Ozburn said, meeting Islix's dark eyes with his own. "To bring both sides peace for the first time in centuries."

Islix nodded to himself, thoughtful in his stare. He was at least glad the two ultimately shared the same goal.

"To share our land with one another is the ultimate resignation of peace between the two kingdoms." The general nodded along.

"And you want to share land as well?" Islix asked.

"But of course, that is what a true alliance means!" General Ozburn laughed, resulting in Islix meeting Aslin's glare beside him.

Hours passed by, with more demands being made of the Indomnis than any compromise. Islix shook his head, a perpetual look of disappointment lining his ever-red flushed face. Even when the two groups thought they were getting somewhere, Ozburn would take everything the two sides had discussed and bring everyone three steps back. Aslin had to stop Islix from storming out at least three times in the span of five hours, their short curly hair barely contained as she held Islix back and mumbled words in their native language to 'let the dumbass get it all out first'.

Ozburn eventually called for a break in the meeting, for everyone to eat and drink before they could continue for the latter portion of talks. A well-deserved few moments away from one another would do the two sides some good.

Islix rolled his eyes when Ozburn wasn't looking, a single sigh of relief leaving him as he stood from his chair and let his soldiers stretch for a while, a few choosing to walk about the castle freely while some stuck around.

When he looked up from his exhausted stupor, he watched one of the maids bringing in beverages to set on the table in front of him.

Islix looked up at her face, meeting with a set of occupied honey eyes, covered by long black curls that he had never seen before, on any human or Indomnis. She set down the remaining drinks that overloaded her arms with a relieving sigh, wiping her forehead of sweat with the back of her hand.

Acting on instinct, Islix couldn't seem to look away until she met his gaze back. Unlike everyone else in the room, her eyes spoke of intrigue and somehow, amusement. He watched her carefully, feeling as though time had stopped around him, unable to manage a single word to come out. She cut her eyes away, looking at the small mess of the Royan side and began to clear up the mess they left behind.

"Do you need me to bring anything else?" She directed her question at the distracted Indomnis general, backing away with various empty cups building up in her hands.

"Do you need help carrying those?" Islix managed to ask in return, but was met with immediate scorn as Ozburn approached from behind the woman.

"The maid can handle it just fine." He said, walking past the two of them, and leaving them be once more to approach Aslin. "Make haste, Zinnia, do not waste our guests' time."

She nodded and went to leave the meeting room, but turned around to find Islix curious eyes and stoic face following her out.

Zinnia flashed a quick smile back, disappearing in the hall before he could return the favor.

Islix struggled to pay full attention in the latter half of the meeting, following the advice of his most trusted friend to simply let the old man get all of his grievances out. While Islix wanted to voice his absolute disdain for this idea, he also couldn't fight against it. The two kingdoms had a lot of recovering to do before any talk of a deep and true alliance could be established.

In fact, Islix left the meeting with an idea of how he would organize his own. With the help of his soldiers later that night in the comfort of his own home, he would compile every issue, every scorn, and every grievance, and confront each of them to find an end.

Perhaps change could be possible.

II

On the second day of the alliance meeting between the Indomnis and Royan kingdoms, Islix woke up just before dawn, ready to tackle the problems that had collected over a century of disputes and arguments. He went around to each of his soldiers, collecting evidence and documenting everything they had experienced at the hands of the opposing side. With the help of his trusted few, he was able to organize and properly put into words every transgression enacted by the Royan kingdom. Every moment in which this army had acted against his own, the goal being to place everything out in the open to properly discuss and mediate, once and for all.

He prepared everything to the finest detail he could, exhausted but proud of what he had achieved.

Islix showed up with his small group of soldiers at the castle of Royan, his list of incidents and grievances ready.

When the two groups finally did their introductions and sat down, the general of the Royan army took control of the conversation almost immediately.

"With the second day's meeting, I believe it is time to discuss points in which both the Royan and the Indomnis militaries would assist one another."

"General Ozburn, if I may suggest something before we enter a different category."

"Nonsense, military talks are of absolute importance." Ozburn simply brushed him off.

"I do not wish to move on when you took all of yesterday to discuss your issues with the Indomnis without giving us the same time and attention to allow us the same opportunity."

"Must we bring up the past after we had already done so yesterday?" Ozburn raised a brow.

"Excuse me?" Islix blinked his black eyes profusely, willing his heart to slow down from the speed it began taking.

"I thought all the problems of the past were already discussed. What more is there?"

"Well," Islix took out his carefully made list of handwritten pages, ready to give him the answer to that. "A lot actually. We of the Indomnis would like to go over every transgression of the Royan and air our grievances over the past century in a mediated discussion. In order to properly conduct business with one another, you must listen and acknowledge these transgressions, to put them behind us. Speaking up on these topics will lead to a stronger alliance, do you not agree?"

"That is not necessary." Ozburn retorted, briefly waving his hand.

Aslin stood up from their chair, looking the opposing general in the eye. "It is absolutely necessary."

"You dare interrupt your own leader?" Ozburn's tone began to increase, but Islix put his hand up to stop him.

"Do not raise your tone with us, they are more trusted than my own blood." Islix's voice raised, a scowl pointing at the general's reaction. He took a glance at Ozburn's own soldiers and recognized the unmistakable look of fear in all their eyes. "Aslin, please continue." Islix encouraged, his voice softening.

Aslin's intense expression softened with encouragement from their leader. "As you were saying before, Islix. I believe it to be crucial for both sides to speak plainly with one another. Having been here yesterday, I think it is obvious that the Royan kingdom has taken more than enough of their time doing so on their end. And not to be personal, but I would never agree to an alliance with the kingdom that swore for our genocide at the beginning of the century, if they are not willing to admit their own mistakes." They finished, prolonging eye contact with General Ozburn in the process without as much as a blink.

Islix and his other soldiers nodded and clamored in agreement. He looked up and down the long table, a smile crossed his red complexion. A part of him felt proud to be a leader of such a strong people, but especially so knowing the Indomnis could feel comfortable speaking their mind with him present. His confidence rose and he straightened his back, a part of him more than ready to be at the defense of his people. The collection of soldiers on his side of the table lined the room with their various shades of red complexions and various sized horns, some with thin black tails settled to their sides.

"Ozburn of the Royan kingdom, you *will* hear us out, so long as you seek a treaty and alliance from the Indomnis. This is not negotiable." Islix insisted, knowing the fate of his people rested on his own civility as well as his fortitude with the others seated across from him.

"Let us begin then." Ozburn sighed, relinquishing the next four hours to the list in front of Islix, lined with multiple occurrences of unprovoked attacks on his people, his family, and even himself. He made sure to keep the confidentiality of each of his own soldiers, only disregarding it when a few had risen to testify their own recounts. With some on the list, others on his side had spoken up sporadically. Islix couldn't help but feel a growing weight in his chest as this part of the meeting had gone on for far longer than either general expected.

This only made his need for justice rise more.

Islix refused any offer for a break until every single part of his list, until every single person had spoken to their completion. He watched as Ozburn grew more and more tired with each spoken occurrence.

By the time both groups disbanded for the night, Islix had been there until sunset. Hesitantly, Ozburn offered a part of the castle to the Indomnis to reside in for the time being while the two kingdoms continued their discussions for alliance. Islix easily accepted his offer, refusing to make his soldiers do the hour-long walk back and forth to the Royan castle twice a day.

Passing through the wing of the castle Islix and the other Indomnis were granted, the moon seemed to settle more light in the area than the barely burning sconces along the walls of the hallway.

But he still saw her clear as day.

Zinnia walked alone through the hall, only stopping a few feet away when she realized someone shared the hallway with her.

"I apologize, I did not realize anyone was staying in this wing, or would even still be awake so late in the night." She bowed her head and tried to walk past him, but Islix put an arm out in front of her.

"Zinnia, correct?"

"You do not have to call me that." Her tender voice hesitated, keeping her eyes forward to the other end of the hall. She felt his keen gaze remain on her.

"Is that not your name?" He asked with a strange sincerity.

"It is." She said quietly, with more ready to leave her mouth, but otherwise left unsaid.

"Zinnia then," Islix unknowingly let a smile slip from his lips. "I never got a chance to say thank you for the other day."

Her honeypot eyes drifted up at him with surprise. "What for?"

"Bringing the drinks. It was very much needed." He tilted his head to the side, taking in the suddenly flushed look on her cheeks.

"No need to thank me for doing my job." She held her breath as she felt a strain of a smile on her face, but fought it back for the sake of professionalism.

"Then it sounds like I shall see you again tomorrow."

"Perhaps. If you take a break next time." She chuckled, the sound warming his chest. "I must say, you took quite the stance today. Ozburn is reeling as we speak, but I too...think it was necessary for him to hear everything." Her voice softened, a part of her hoping no one had heard her say that.

"As do I." Islix agreed before realizing one very important detail. "Did you watch the meeting?"

Zinnia hesitantly nodded, knowing she very well could be scolded. But she was instead met with the same gentle smile as she was yesterday.

"I see." Islix acknowledged with a brief nod.

"Hopefully tomorrow, what you will witness will be less confrontational."

"I hope so, too. Peace between the Indomnis and Royan has been needed for a long time." Zinnia felt warmth on her face flourish. "Islix, yes?"

He put down his outstretched arm, partly tempted to reach his hand out to her small face. The sound of his name from her mouth felt destined to be, as if it were natural. And part of him wished to hear it again and again.

"Yes." Islix managed to breathe out, fighting back his own flustered expression.

"I hope you succeed, Islix. Perhaps keep that between us?" Her coy smile followed her as she walked past him, hurrying down to the other end of the hall, and carefully down the crumbling stone stairs.

Islix made his way to his room for the night and decided to utilize his art skills for the remainder of the night, until he found himself ready to sleep. His heart never returned to the beat it once held.

Because Zinnia suddenly held it in her particularly anxious hands.

III

Night had turned to day, before the glow of the late
sun singled for the afternoon.

In the late stay of yet another meeting between the
Royan and Indomnis people, Islix yearned for a
change in topic, overwhelmed by the constant
discussion of the Royan kingdom and their supposed
supremacy compared to the other kingdoms around
them. If he thought the military demands of the
Royan were too much, their latest discussion had
given him a run for his money. He and the rest of the
Indomnis soldiers on his side sat in a collective silence,
their faces flush with exhaustion, needing a break from
General Ozburn and his unfortunately persistent but
dull voice.

Today, Ozburn spoke of expectations and terms of
what the two people could accomplish together. But
more so, what and how the Indomnis would benefit
from an alliance with the Royan, not allowing any
room for the Indomnis general to introduce anything
to the conversation. General Ozburn found himself
repeating the same ideas from earlier, repetitive in his

belief that the Royan kingdom surpassed everyone else around them in both military and political power. The single hour had turned into two, then three, his words becoming more of a tangent than anything else.

Even Aslin was on the brink of falling asleep, her pitch black eyes ready to roll up far into the back of her head, never to return again. Islix gently nudged her with his elbow, prompting her to straighten herself in the chair from her leaned back position.

"In the last century, the Royan kingdom has had its differences with those around us, but for good reason," General Ozburn began. "For the world may move forward in time, our traditions and beliefs should not be so quick to veer away from its roots. Those around us do not seem to want to uphold the ways of the old, leaving the Royan kingdom the last line of defense when it comes to maintaining the glory of our origins, of our empire." He said, shifting his hand into a fist on the table in front of him.

"Have you considered that change might bring you into a new era that could positively influence your kingdom?" Islix asked with genuine curiosity.

"That is why we have invited the Indomnis kingdom to our castle, to do just that." General Ozburn nodded, his eyes shifting to the left at the Royan coat of arms mounted on the wall. "I think an

alliance speaks for itself with benefits to both sides."
He stated, flipping his papers downward so its
contents could not be seen by any prying eyes.

"I can see why." Islix nodded, a respectful smile
crossing his face.

"Then we should end the meeting on this note:
Considering all we can offer the Indomnis." Ozburn
stood from his seat, nodding once to Islix who stood
seconds after. The two shook hands briefly, but
Ozburn kept hold of the other general's hand. "Islix,
would you care to follow me for a moment, to speak
from one general to another?"

Islix rose a brow before rising from his seat,
reluctantly accepting his offer. He looked down to
Aslin's concerned face, both exchanging a short nod
before walking off with the Royan general.

He followed him out the southernmost door,
trying to keep up as the older general crossed through
the empty dining room, not much to note within it
besides a set of metal armor on display by each door. A
long table similar to the one in the meeting room sat
void of anything except for a mostly melted
candelabra. A layer of dust caked on the armor by the
incoming set of doors, and on the various paintings
depicting sceneries from within the castle itself, of

moments far before Islix's time. The emptiness of the room caught his attention, save for the table itself.

Ozburn walked Islix through a set of identical doors, into a much too small room. He shut the door behind them, lighting the sconces on each wall. The room's biggest section of wall across from them was filled with mounted swords of all different shapes and sizes, staffs and spears alike lining the wall to his left, while various shields of various kingdoms' coats of arms colored each of them individually. One in particular took his attention, a black base with red poppy flowers faded across the metal.

Islix reached out to touch it before Ozburn took his attention away.

"Behold; the Royan kingdom's treasure room!" General Ozburn exclaimed, pride swelling in his voice. Islix took his hand back, holding his breath.

"Impressive." He managed to breathe out.

"Centuries of strife, among neighbors close and far, have brought us to this very moment. I think you understand with our changing world, we need one another more than ever before."

Islix tore his eyes away from the shield, meeting with Ozburn's stationary blue eyes. He stood tall beside the Indomnis shield mounted on the wall, worn and faded from war, feeling as if it were calling out to him in that brief moment.

"General Ozburn, I think we need peace, far more than anything else." Islix insisted, stepping toward him. "War need not be on the horizon for a long time to come between any neighboring kingdom, so long as we respect those around us. I truly believe that peace can be achieved between the Indomnis and Royan kingdoms, that it should be a priority."

"Peace is an option, so long as the Indomnis can fight alongside us when the time comes." Ozburn watched Islix carefully, his nod bringing some semblance of understanding.

"I think this can be arranged."

When General Ozburn led the two of them out of the room, he shook his hand once more before taking his leave for the night. Islix breathed out a sigh of relief, slowly retreating back towards the wing of the Royan castle the Indomnis inhabited. On his walk back, he encountered Aslin and a few other soldiers talking amongst themselves in the meeting room. She quickly made her way to his side, her face brimming with frustration, complaints ready to spill out.

"Sometimes I wonder if he understands other kingdoms exist." Aslin complained, stretching out her back until a crack came from her efforts.

"Agreed." Islix yawned, his eyes following the door, expectant in a way. The look was caught by Aslin, who raised her brows knowingly.

"No sign of your maid friend from before?" She commented, a scornful stare leaving Islix. "Maybe next time then? It is fairly late." She shrugged.

"Who knows?" Islix muttered under his breath, leading the two of them out of the room.

The Indomnis duo left the now candlelit meeting room from the southern door, making their way up the stairs and into the long hall. Passing through another door to the north of the dining room, they ended up in the common room. The area was large in both height and width, able to fit close to a hundred people comfortably. The high arched ceiling was made with articulate stonework, while the walls held various weapons and occasionally burnt out sconces on its walls, some untouched and others with faded blades and scuffs. The uneven cobblestone floor was far more barren, a few spaces discolored, seeming as though they once held furniture at one point or another. Single doors sat on every wall, save for the wooden double doors leading out to the Royan castle gardens.

Oddly enough, the room held quite the mixture of soldiers from both sides, each separated with their own kingdom's soldiers.

"Strange to see so many people still awake after all of that." Aslin commented, quickly addressing the nearest Indomnis soldier. "Why is everyone gathered this late?"

"The night sky has changed hue. I didn't believe it until I saw the change for myself." He smiled, a touch giddy.

Islix and Aslin shared an uncertain look with one another before heading out of the courtyard entrance, leading to a balcony full of uneven but eroded stone, similar to the floor inside. They both looked up, staring off at the night sky with, indeed, a plethora of red and green ribbons of light shifting ever so slightly if they focused their eyes enough.

"Islix, this is an aurora. I cannot believe I would be alive for one of these." Aslin's eyes drifted off into the atmosphere, not daring to blink just yet.

Islix watched the gentle shifts in colors, how the stars still clustered through the vibrant reds, reminiscent of his skin tone. It was a beauty unlike anything he has ever seen before.

A short tap of his shoulder from Aslin stole his attention, her gaze narrowed towards the overgrowth below and further away from the two of them. When his eyes readjusted, he spotted Zinnia sitting alone on the high grass, her knees pulled up to her chest. Her large eyes set on the phenomenon above them.

Without a second thought, Islix made his way down the stairs, setting his path towards Zinnia. He walked around bunches of closed wildflowers, doing his best to disturb as little of the gardens as possible. Before he could reach her, she turned her head towards the rustling sounds of his boots, a short smile crossing her lips as she adjusted her long skirt further over her knees.

"Come to watch the night sky with a better view?" Her soft voice chimed in, gentle and sweet all at once.

Islix towered over her even more now than that she was seated, leaving him briefly self-conscious. "If you would like my company." He responded back.

"That would be fine with me." She looked to the spot beside her, then back at him.

Islix sat beside her, his eyes settling back on the tapestry of colors above them. He enjoyed the way the night sky shifted, how every second was different from the last.

"It is unlike anything I have ever witnessed before." Islix breathed, breaking the silence between them.

Zinnia sighed, her eyes never once leaving their place in the ever-shifting aurora.

He pushed part of his hair from the left to the right, fixing the few strands stuck over his horns. The nerves bundling together inside his chest weighed more now than ever before. Islix sat as still as he could, so as not to disturb Zinnia beside him.

He peered to his left, watching the colors dance in her eyes. The dark honey color mixed with the red, leaving a gentle glow in them. For a better part of his time beside her, Islix found his gaze drifting back to her, sneaking glances at her before she turned to catch his stare.

"Enjoying the view?" She asked, looking to the strange aurora above them.

"Every minute." He watched her carefully as he answered. "There is nothing greater than the beauty of nature."

"Absolutely." Zinnia sighed, settling her head onto her knees.

"Are you cold? You are in uniform in the middle of the night."

"I'll be fine, no need to worry about me." She broke her eyes away from the sky, glancing at Islix.

He nodded, but as time passed, he couldn't help noting her occasional shakes, seemingly suppressing her shivers as they came. He instantly slipped off his coat, settling the heavy fabric over her shoulders. He wore a meager leather chest piece, hugging the muscle and ripples on his chest, all the way down to his waist. Revealing more of the faded crimson red of his skin.

Neither said much of anything to one another for the next hour, though Islix was pleased to see Zinnia settle into his coat and noticed her shivers ceased.

His eyes continued to wander from the dancing lights above him to the silent woman at his side, unable to focus on the aurora for too long.

"Is that better?" He asked, already knowing the answer.

"Yes, thank you. Are you sure you don't need your coat?" Zinnia nodded hesitantly, but her wondrous eyes did not break their concentration.

"Not at all. Indomnis have a certain tolerance for the cold. Well, more so than humans." He shrugged.

"Impressive. So you don't feel the cold in the winter?"

"Barely. Likely contributed as to why the Royan kingdom had a habit of calling us devils for so long." Islix leaned back in his seat before feeling a small hand touch his own. Zinnia looked up at him, her sad eyes more apologetic than General Ozburn's after being told of a lifetime of atrocities.

"You are no devil to me, Islix. I'm sorry anyone is awful enough to say that to you." She said, feeling the warmth of his hand beneath hers.

In her small apology, Islix still felt her sincerity.

He wondered to himself how he had never met a person so understanding. Someone who saw him as he was within, not for the features that he wore.

He looked down and slowly upturned his hand, feeling the cold of her palm in the warmth of his own.

"If only you were the one sitting across from me every day. These meetings would be far more peaceful and productive." Islix laughed, prompting Zinnia to shy away.

"I am no mediator." She mumbled timidly.

"Too bad." He enclosed his hand around hers, rubbing his thumb over her hand to restore some level of heat to her cold hand.

Islix and Zinnia returned their eyes to the sky, allowing the night sky to paint itself in colors as the two of them sat hand in hand, until the very last light faded away hours later.

IV

After the time they shared in the castle gardens, watching the lights dance above one another, Islix's coat was returned, scented with flowers so reminiscent of Zinnia. He did not dare take it off throughout the entire meeting the next day, from its late start onward.

Words blurred from Ozburn's mouth. For Islix, the opposing generals' tangents went into one ear and out the next. The longer these meetings became, the more Islix questioned his choice to agree to a treaty at all. The same man who initiated the alliance lacked the ability to properly conduct his less than coherent thoughts when speaking to the room, seemingly repeating the same thoughts on the previous war between the Royan kingdom and one of their neighbors to the north, over and over again.

Islix let out a deep breath as he willed himself to listen. A part of him sat unsure if he were simply distracted or if General Ozburn had been slowly trailing off topic the last few meetings.

But even so, the entire prospect of an alliance began to feel a bit further whenever he and the rest of the Indomnis were forced to listen to whatever war story had decided to leave General Ozburn's mouth on this day. An early break was very much needed.

And Islix would do whatever he needed to achieve this.

In one abrupt movement, he stood from his chair, causing the other general to pause his latest tale of conquest and might.

Islix settled his dark eyes on him and forced a peaceful smile across his notably irritable expression. "I think you make some great points, General Ozburn. However, I feel as though we may have accidentally trailed off into some more minor, unnecessary areas. How about the two of us take the afternoon to realign our goals for this potential alliance?" Islix chose his words carefully, hoping not to give the other general the impression that he wanted to cut the meeting short.

Even if that was indeed his entire intention.

Islix and the other Indomnis soldiers waited patiently as General Ozburn's face shifted from intent thought to something akin to agreement. Everyone held their breath until he finally spoke.

"I suppose that could help us realign our goals. Shall we reconvene in the morning with our thoughts?"

"Absolutely." Islix agreed, looking to Aslin, whose face spoke of nothing less than exhaustion. She stood beside Islix, as the two generals ended their latest meeting with a shake of hands before disbanding for the day.

Islix felt a weight lift from his body, feeling a sense of freedom from the tense discussions of possible alliances with such questionable people. At this rate, he would need to seriously reconsider if continuing the discussions were an honest path to peace or if he were simply being treated a fool.

Introspection was needed before he could keep going.

Islix quickly took his second in command's attention, leaning close to Aslin's ear as he left them in charge until he returned. There was no way to clear his mind while stuck inside the dank, crumbling halls of the Royan castle. Islix made his way out of the room, utilizing the same path from last night. He went through the double doors into the courtyard, following the barely viable path set out before him. Fresh soil only adorned one side of the worn path, while the remainder was overgrown with various shrubbery. Uneven patches of grass and wildflowers spawning everywhere around him and occasionally, on the path he walked.

He found himself In a more remote part of the courtyard, if he was even still in the same area at all. Islix walked through more of a forested area, but felt as though he weren't alone.

"Islix!" A sudden sprint from the grass came towards him and forced Islix to turn around, noticing the small, familiar figure coming into view. The same black skirt and blue apron wrapped around her chest approached him, barely able to stand straight when she caught up to him.

"Zinnia? What are you doing so far from the castle?" Islix placed a hand on her shoulder, kneeling beside her while she attempted to catch her breath. Her pale cheeks stung with pink from her run. She breathed heavily, still unable to speak.

"Take your time." Islix pulled the hair over her face back behind her shoulder, revealing more of her warm face. Part of her shifted back, embarrassment showing itself on her expression.

"I thought I had more stamina than that." Zinnia finally said, her voice hoarse.

Islix held back the laughter building in his throat, revealing only a smile.

"Is there a reason you ran all the way out here?" He inquired once more.

Zinnia struggled to catch her breath, unable to respond for a brief minute or so.

But when she finally regained her ability to properly speak, she took in the warm, spring air in a single breath.

"I saw you wandering off and I was worried you would get lost." Zinnia admitted, the words slipping out with a tinge of uncertainty to them.

"Lost? I did not stray too much from the path." Islix said, thinking aloud. "Though this is quite the mess. Do you not have someone to tend to the courtyard?"

"Not anymore. General Ozburn deemed it unnecessary to have a keeper for the flowers. He said it was unimportant compared to the work of a soldier."

"The more I hear about him, the less I am surprised."

Zinnia met his worried stare with one of her own. A question burned in her thoughts, yearning to come out before stopping herself. Her hands tightened into fists beside her, before nervously settling on the hem of her skirt. She looked out around them before finally letting her curiosity slip.

"What made you want to accept General Ozburn's offer for alliance, if you don't mind me asking?" She straightened herself out, smoothing out her hair as if it didn't take all her strength to ask such a simple sounding question.

Islix thought to himself for a moment, making sure to think out his answer.

He supposed it was after everything the Indomnis went through at the hands of the Royan kingdom. It was not just his generation who had suffered, but his father, and his father before him. For much of his childhood, he wondered if peace would ever be found in his lifetime. It left him vowing to make those changes himself, were he to gain status as a leader. And now, here he was, listening to the Royan general drone on and on about the battles and wars he vested himself into.

He recalled the worn shield in the treasure room, its faded scars haunting him.

Exasperated, Islix huffed.

"I suppose I think violence between the two people is unnecessary. I have always felt strongly about that. But no one else is willing to bridge that gap, save for myself and General Ozburn, it seems." Islix said, watching Zinnia's face light up at his words.

"I think that is very noble of you." Zinnia looked off at the overgrown path ahead, her eyes following the route ahead. "Not many would be so willing to go out of their way to fix hundreds of years of violence."

"I would not say I am noble yet. I am simply trying my best."

"I can see that. I would still say that makes you very noble."

Islix felt his face warm up at the compliment. It was strange for him, but he was suddenly speechless. Her wandering eyes found him once more.

"Would you want to see at least one part of the garden that remained kept with?" Zinnia offered him a distraction, putting her hands together over her apron.

Islix met her excited eyes with a nod, instantly letting her lead him deeper into the overgrowth, down a short corridor of overbearing maple trees, barely giving him room to maneuver as she took his hand. The two made it out to the other side, revealing a part of the outer castle border, barely upheld with the massive crumbling stones that made up the wall.

But below it on the ground, where no one would expect, bloomed a long line of multicolored roses. A deep red made up the majority of the flowers, but a few tinged with lighter and darker hues of the same color. Nearest the end of the line of flowers before becoming general overgrowth again were flowers closer to black.

To say Islix was surprised was an understatement.

"Zinnia, are these your doing?" He asked, feeling her hand let go of his.

"No, certainly not. They were here long before me. But, with a combined effort, myself and two other maids have been making sure to water and care for them, nothing more, nothing less. Now more bloomed this year compared to previous ones. It is truly impressive how resilient these flowers can be."

"Indeed." Islix said, his eyes not leaving Zinnia's smiling face. How such a view could compel his heart back onto the right path, he was unsure.

Before Islix and Zinnia left the area by the castle wall, he took a moment to clear up some of the weeds growing around the flowers, being sure to avoid the thorns protruding from the surrounding stems. The two began their walk back, the gentle warmth of the sun lost on the thick branches above them. Lost in thought, Islix almost didn't notice Zinnia begin to trip over a fallen branch, covered by excess brush. He caught her arm before she could fall over, grabbing the edge of his coat to steady herself.

"Are you okay, Zinnia?" Islix held onto her arm, his tight grip easing from her partly pulled back long sleeve. A small, discolored scar made itself visible momentarily before leaving his line of sight. He didn't let her go, nor did she, finding herself surveying his face, a single glance spent on his lips.

Zinnia shook off her thoughts and straightened herself out, feeling Islix's gaze settle on her as she felt his hand settle on the small of her back, between the hem of her skirt and blouse. He moved with only instinct, cornering her against the crumbling wall, his first overhead. He leaned in close, not daring to blink, fearful of missing a single second of her curious honey eyes.

"Do you know how much I adore you, Zinnia?" Islix's voice rang through the short distance between them. "No other human could compare. Not with you." He tilted her chin up, drinking the flustered expression growing on her face.

"Islix," Zinnia's tender annunciation pushed his heart over the edge, bridging the gap between them. His lips met with her cheek, leaving gentle kiss after kiss until he reached her ear. "What if someone found us like this?" Her hand hesitantly touched his chest ever so slightly, before his clasped over it, leaning close.

"Then let them watch." Islix whispered into her ear. He kissed the side of her face before her earlobe, feeling her unsteady breath leave her lips.

Zinnia pulled his face back, stealing a kiss from him when he least expected it. Islix responded in kind, threading his hand from the side of her face through her hair. He felt nothing less than need course through him, pressing her against the wall with all his strength. Bold and in the moment, his lips mended perfectly with hers, ready to explore every part his tongue could reach.

In turn, Zinnia allowed Islix dominion over every part of her he could reach. Every touch remained gentle and patient, never daring to be anything less. He felt the heat of her flushed cheeks beneath his hand, caressing the soft skin to bring him closer. All he wanted was to keep her close, yearning for her presence ever since the two of them first crossed paths.

The subtle closeness between them was nothing less than addictive. Islix pulled Zinnia close to him, enveloping her waist between his arms. He didn't dare leave an inch between them, growing more and more desperate with each kiss.

"Islix." She murmured against his lips, prompting his pause. He smiled, the sound of his name leaving her lips tempting him even more before he kissed her cheek. "We should go back, before anyone notices. What if someone needs you?" Zinnia blinked, her honey eyes staring with growing concern.

Islix felt his mood drop. She made a valid point. Even so, he didn't want to leave just yet.

"Always so selfless." Islix muttered, leaving a stray kiss to her forehead.

"Not at all." She retorted quietly, staring down at the ground. Islix tightened his arms around her, before hesitantly letting go. Her hands clasped together over her skirt, finding her strength to meet his gaze again. "Ready to go back?"

"Never, but lead the way." He said, following close behind her.

"Thank you for coming along with me today." She smiled, letting her arm slip out his hand and back to her side before continuing down the path back towards the castle. Islix hesitated before following her back, his unsettled thoughts keeping him silent for a time. That was, until he was prompted by Zinnia with questions.

The two spoke of flowers and politics on the way back, leaving Islix's renewed resolve to settle him back into his mindset of obtaining peace between both the Indomnis and the Royan kingdoms.

V

Another day meant another meeting between the Indomnis and Royan kingdoms, to collaborate in an attempt for peace and prosperity between the two.

Or so, Islix thought.

General Ozburn had started the meeting off by requesting access to the resources of the Indomnis kingdom, citing his need as a right, as if they had agreed upon this earlier on.

"Bringing up the metal deposits will not dissuade me from openly noting the problems you keep pushing away, General Ozburn." Islix spoke calmly, forcing his face to maintain its stoic look. "I have told you my stance on the matter. I will not grant access to these resources unless the two kingdoms have fully resolved everything and we have achieved an agreed upon non aggression pact."

At one point in time, the two sides had gotten out their issues with one another, making mention of plenty of moments in time in which the Royan people transgressed on Indomnis land and their people. This part took far longer, as Islix took the time to make sure that each and every single one of his people could be heard, to voice their grief, as well as his own, with those who caused it.

However, Ozburn was a stubborn man. He took a few moments of their meeting to fight back a handful of the accusations, stating their alleged state, not even treating the incidents with a hint of legitimacy. At other times, Ozburn would simply wave off these issues, but Islix refused to back down.

Almost at perfect timing, the two leaders sat at a stalemate halfway through their meeting, agreeing to take a break from discussions.

Islix grew tired just looking at General Ozburn. To grant him any rights this early on would be idiotic, as both a leader and a fighter for peace.

His energy only returned when their break began and he saw Zinnia enter the room once more, bringing with her a tray full of drinks. Her long sleeved black uniform stretched over her body in the form of a black skirt far over her knees, and flat black shoes to match. She set down one tray before retrieving a second one outside of the room. The only colorful piece on her was a pale blue apron over her chest, tied behind her back. To his luck, Ozburn had even left the meeting room with his soldiers, leaving Islix and Zinnia to be somewhat left alone unlike the time prior.

He shuffled around in his coat pocket, taking out a folded piece of paper meant for her, but when he did locate it, suddenly his anxiety rose with her quick approach and he second-guessed himself.

Zinnia looked tired as she did before, but the exhaustion seemed to melt away into a short smile when she looked up for Islix, who practically returned it tenfold.

Aslin had been talking to one of the soldiers in the corner of the room when she turned to see what the other had been looking at. The two of them kept the comments to themselves, but neither contained their snickering much, watching their leader be very clearly smitten with the short human in front of him.

"You truly have the best timing, Zinnia." Islix smiled, helping her unload the many plain silver cups in her hands. "Care to join us today?" He asked, the bold request slipping out before he could think twice.

Zinnia placed the other cups beside her down, meeting his overly confident grin with her own humble look. "Maids are not allowed to sit on the job." She said matter-of-factly, a bit too obviously disappointed in the rule.

"Ozburn is not around to stop you. Besides, I am his equal." Islix excused, getting up from his seat to offer it to Zinnia. She hesitated for a moment before obliging, watching Islix prop himself up on the table to sit across from her, taking the mug in front of him to drink from. "If he has any complaints, I will say it is a custom and claim my confusion if told otherwise." He grinned happily, making a face at his own plan. She giggled, a short skip of Islix's heart memorizing the sound.

"I suppose I should take a moment to assist the Indomnis and assure their comforts are being met. How are your talks going?" Zinnia inquired quietly as she pulled up her long sleeves, settling into the warm chair and placing her hands flat in her lap.

"We have seen better days." Islix shook off the thought of having to return to the meeting soon. "Though my day becomes far better with company like yours around." Islix pushed his dark hair to one side over his shoulder, hoping his comment would be well received.

Zinnia's surprise turned to a subtle blush creeping around her face, making it a point to avoid his dark eyes pointed in her direction.

"I suppose I could say the same when I come here." When she met his eyes again, he seemed to breathe out in relief, before he fumbled for something in his coat pocket.

"Open your hand for me." He spoke quickly, her small hand outstretched between them, opening without much thought. He placed the small folded up paper in her hands, before closing it up with his own.

"What is it?" She didn't dare move her hand, letting the warmth of his palm overtake her cold hand.

"For later." His voice lingered as he drew close to her ear, not noticing his soldiers in the background watching him.

What he did notice though, had him ready to ask her questions. Small bruises lined her wrist and forearm, fairly new compared to the ones he spotted yesterday on her pale skin. His inspection of her arm became far too obvious, and Zinnia stole back her hand, pulling down the sleeve of her uniform over her arms.

Before he could get another word out, Zinnia had abruptly stood up and left as General Ozburn entered the room, redder in the face than before and immediately ready to continue.

Islix didn't have much of an attention span to focus on the now fumbling Ozburn, his mind elsewhere for some time during their meeting. His worry outshined any and all of the partially drunken string of words coming from the general's mouth, until he could no longer take it.

"General Ozburn of the Royan kingdom, are your drunken rambles finished yet or should we pick up again when you have found sobriety?"

Before the opposing general could interrupt, Islix called for an abrupt end to the meeting for the night, citing his reason being his ability to see that Ozburn refused to take him or the problems that the Royan people inflicted on the Indomnis seriously.

Partly sulking from the awful end to the meeting, Islix found his focus returned onto Zinnia. Crossing through almost pitch black hallways on his way to his room, he stopped in the middle of the hall right outside of his door, hoping to encounter Zinnia once more. He remembered her shy smile, the small hand of hers staying within his own, thinking of everything about her that took up space in his mind.

The note he left in her hand was a sketch of a zinnia flower among a field of grass. Or at least, with his lacking artistic skills, he hoped she would see it as it was intended.

Islix found himself flustered again, the sound of her soft voice saying his name temporarily taking the place of all other worries.

While standing in front of his room, he wondered if he should make something else. Or, if Aslin would comment on his odd behavior again. Or perhaps, his close friend would use it as ammunition to poke fun at him again at a later time.

Islix dreamt of a field of lush, pre-blooming flowers, of the night sky above them with the very same lights both him and Zinnia had watched together a few nights prior. The feeling of her hand in his was more of a sensation than reality, but adding to the warmth in his chest. He only wished it did not end so soon.

In the middle of the cast of flowers, sat a single black zinnia, swaying with the wind.

VI

Islix woke up the next morning, thinking of his dream. The weight in his chest returned when he realized he had to wake up and return to the meeting room. Another day meant more of General Ozburn and his interesting viewpoints.

But Islix showed up dressed in his suit of thin black armor, covering only his torso and legs with layers of leather, his coat not needed on such a warm day. He took a moment in front of the mirror, fixing back his long hair in dual braids meeting at the back of his head, and tied it off with a red ribbon. He pushed a few stray black hairs away from his horns, dusting off his thin armor, and ready to deal with everything coming his way, all for the future of his people.

When he arrived at the meeting room, Indomnis soldiers began to trickle in slowly. One by one, they all sat around, waiting for some kind of sign from the Royan soldiers and their beloved general. Minutes turned into an hour, leaving everyone wondering where the general could be.

One of the Indomnis soldiers was handed a note from another outside of the room, shrugging as he walked over to hand it to Islix. With no context, Islix hesitantly unraveled the note.

Within the same piece of paper he had drawn on two nights ago stood a sunflower beside the zinnia, though far taller and wider than the now tiny flower.

Islix placed a hand over his mouth as he stared at the piece of paper, feeling his cheeks burn. He really didn't expect a response from this, let alone an addition to his original piece. Aslin had looked over his shoulder before seating themself beside him, nudging his shoulder to gain his attention.

"Zinnia?" Aslin asked, pumping their eyebrows up. Islix nodded, folding the piece of paper and putting it away in his chest pocket.

"Cute. Stupid, but cute." Aslin added.

As the meeting came to a later than typical start, Islix noticed once again that General Ozburn had shown up red faced and barely coherent, somehow worse off than the night prior.

Before letting him begin to speak after their shared traditional introductions, Islix shook his head and found himself speaking out of turn.

"Why are you inebriated during another meeting?" Islix asked, not even giving him the chance to sit down.

"What do you mean?" Ozburn shot back. The soldiers beside him all seemed far worse for wear than they were before, catching not only Islix's attention, but that of everyone on his side. Aslin looked to their leader with concern, both for the safety of the Indomnis and the Royan soldiers alike.

"I am concerned your current state will not accomplish anything. Have you been drinking through the night into the morning?" He asked, already knowing the answer.

For the first time since the arrival of the Indomnis, a Royan soldier spoke out of turn and stepped forward.

"Please forgive his...behavior." They said quietly. "He has been stricken with worry over the alliance between the Royan and Indomnis kingdoms. We will take him to rest, do whatever you will for the remainder of the day. Let us convene another day." The group of Royan soldiers walked the other general out, a collective unity no one expected on the Indomnis side.

"A day off?" Aslin said, eyeballing Islix and pressing their elbow into his side. "I don't suppose you have any idea what you could be doing with that time." They said in a mocking tone.

"Aslin." He whispered, trying to hush them.

"No idea what you could be doing." They commented again, feeling the eyes of a few other Indomnis on Islix.

"I know, I know." He stood up, rolling his pitch-black eyes at them, smoothing down his hair as he left the room.

Islix roamed the halls of the castle in the daylight for the first time, in search of Zinnia. He crept into every light bearing hall, every staircase, into quite a few more rooms than he would like to admit. Before he knew it, he walked by the courtyard doors, and spotted her sweeping the balcony area outside.

When Islix approached, Zinnia's eyes lit up, placing down her broom against the stone of the balcony overlooking the lower garden.

"Islix? I thought you were in a meeting with General Ozburn today, what brings you here?" Her excitement was evident in her bright eyes, leaving Islix elated.

"Ozburn was inebriated, worse than the night prior. Meetings cannot be held unless both parties are sober. A bare basic, but not to all, I suppose." Islix stepped closer, noticing their drastic difference in height. A part of him was sensitive about the way he towered over Zinnia, before he remembered the small drawing in his pocket. "I received your message." He said, voice soft yet full of joy.

"Ah, I'm glad. I was worried I couldn't match your craftsmanship." She smiled back, clasping her hands together. "What are you planning to do for the day then?"

Islix wanted to say so many things at once, but all he could do was stare blankly at her, unsure what to say.

Zinnia laughed, the sound so fleeting, Islix wanted to bottle it up. Her eyes traveled to his back, noticing a large blackwood bow and a quiver attached to his side. "Have you considered archery in the garden?"

"Hm? This old thing?" Islix took out his bow, her eyes widening as she got closer to look at its details. Fine lines showed aging but a few carved spots on the handles leather strap had her in awe.

"I don't believe I've seen a bow so large before. It's quite the thing, isn't it?" Zinnia's eyes looked over every detail.

"Bow needed to be fitted for someone of my stature, so it was quite literally made for me." He quickly handed it off to her. "Would you like to try it?"

Zinnia pondered for a second, her face ready to say yes in a heartbeat, but shied away. "I might break it, I'm no good with these things."

"That is quite alright." He quickly placed it down beside him. "Have you swung a sword around before?" Islix took his entire sheathe from his body, presenting it to Zinnia.

"Islix, can I be candid for a moment?" She asked, his heart sinking at the question. But she leaned in close, signaling for him to bend down. When he did, her next words surprised him. "I have always wanted to swing a sword, can we do that instead?" She backed up, her honey eyes blinking up at him with fascination.

"Absolutely." Islix placed his bow around his back, letting Zinnia lead them both off into the overgrown gardens down the crumbling stairs, away from the castle. The further out into the gardens they got, the more Zinnia grew timid as she overthought her strange request.

Islix slid his hand over hers as she walked ahead, his massive hand overtaking hers. She didn't look back at him until the two arrived at a small open ground, full of different heighted grass. "How is this?" She asked, receiving a quick nod of approval.

"Perfect." He said, taking his sword and placing it on the ground beside her. His coat came off next, placing it neatly folded on the grass. "Are you ready for your lesson today?" he asked, a hint of amusement in his voice.

"As ready as ever." She smiled, pulling off her apron and tossing it to the side.

"Well then. Stand in front of me, turn around so your back faces me."

Zinnia nodded and did as he said, feeling the warmth of his chest make light contact with her back, part of his hair brushing her shoulder. His hand fixed the bend in her knees to the proper angle, and before she knew it, she heard the massive sword unsheathe beside them, a grand blade almost as tall as her being placed in her hands.

"Make sure your palm is tight on the hilt." He tightened his hand over hers, keeping her grip safely on the sword. "I want to stress how dangerous a sword can be, if not handled properly. We do not want anything to happen to you, so let us take it slow. Everything is in the wrist." He stressed, letting her go and swing the sword, the blade barely hitting the tree.

"More power, dear Zinnia." He encouraged, keeping a careful eye on her.

She stepped back, propelling herself forward with a swing and a direct hit to the tree. He smiled, watching her learn her way around a sword with a strange swell of pride. As she was readying for another swing, the sword slipped out of her hands, prompting Islix to grab her and pull her back by her waist before it could land at the base of the tree.

Held tight in his arms, Zinnia could feel the heavy thud of his heart against their back.

Islix tightened his arms around her, unwilling to part with her so close to him. He wanted to keep this for as long as possible, worried what would happen if he let her go.

"Are you alright?" Islix asked in a low voice.

Her eyes peered up at him as her hands settled gently over his protective arms. "I'm fine, I promise. Are you okay, Islix?"

He sighed, a deep exhale leaving his chest before words could. "Yes."

"Did I scare you?" She asked jokingly.

"A bit. I forget your strength is nonexistent."

"Rude." She huffed, her hands moving over his, attempting to bring him some sort of comfort. "Islix, I..." Zinnia started, feeling his arms tighten around her waist, as if to draw closer to her. He leaned close to her ear, his warm breath tingling her neck.

"Yes, Zinnia?" His hushed voice asked, almost inviting.

Struggling to get the words out, she placed one of her hands over his. Her hand barely covered half of his, the faded red of his skin beneath her own. Part of her regretted not speaking up during their time in the rose garden, if only to let slip a few meager words.

"I wanted to say this a few days ago," Her hand gently brushed over his in a small back and forth motion. "I enjoy being around you."

"Zinnia." He sighed. Islix nuzzled his face into her neck, a warm exhale of relief leaving him, the warmth almost welcoming on her skin. He placed a hand below her chin and turned her face to him, stealing her lips in a feverish kiss. His tongue ran along the inside of her mouth, tasting every part of her all the way to her throat.

"How much do you enjoy me, Zinnia?" Islix's hand sank down to her belly, beneath the gap of fabric between her blouse and skirt. He rubbed the soft skin, his warm hand alone encircling the entirety of her stomach. Her hand remained on his, her breath uneven as he turned his attention to her neck. Kisses turned into love bites, making sure not to sink his teeth too far into her skin. The most he took between his teeth, Zinnia's breath hitched.

"More than you know, Islix." She breathed out.

"I wonder about that." Islix pressed his face into her neck. His hand shifted further down from her stomach to her abdomen. "Do you want me to keep going, Zinnia?"

"Yes, please." She quietly begged, her face flushed with warmth as his hand descended below her skirt line. He played with the hem of her underwear, sliding his fingers beneath the thin fabric.

A choked back noise left her lips when his fingertips felt for her warmth, pooling beneath his hand. A low growl rumbled in his chest, begging him to keep going. He lived for the sweet heat collecting, taking his time as he gently traced a finger around her folds.

"Islix, please." Zinnia moaned, his hand pausing at the sound of his name.

"Tell me what you want, darling." Islix teased, his hand remaining still. "Anything you want, and it is yours."

"Keep touching me." She confessed, her shy voice resonating in his mind.

Islix let his fingers drag over her clitoris, struggling to control his own needs. A small whimper left her and her knees buckled together, catching her with his arm tightening around her chest.

"I have you." Islix groaned softly, lowering the two of them to the ground. He kept Zinnia steady on his lap, his pants tightened on contact with her. His pointer and middle finger encircled her clitoris and entrance respectively, placing a finger inside her just to feel her reaction.

The wet feeling closing around his fingers left him unable to resist pushing further inside, drinking in her timid moans as if nothing could stop him. He pulled her further into his lap to let his cock rub against her through his pants, resisting the urge to roll his hips into her back.

A distant call for Zinnia came from the entrance to the castle gardens, catching their collective attention. But Islix didn't stop his rhythmic rubbing, placing a hand gently over her mouth. "I refuse to send you back so pent up." Islix muttered into her ear, speeding up his strokes, penetrating more each time.

"Be a good girl and finish for me." He groaned, her muffled moans barely audible through, her hips rolling faster and faster. Desperate whimpers and moans spilled from her, and soon, Islix's hand was covered by her aftermath. He removed his hands from her mouth and skirt, overlapping both arms around her waist.

"Zinnia." Islix spoke softly into her ear. "Have I told you how much I enjoy your name?"

"I had a feeling." She settled further into his lap. "Did you see my response? I'm not the greatest at drawing, but I did my best." Her tired chuckle lingered in the air around them.

"Likewise. And it was lovely, thank you." Islix tightened his arms around her, kissing the blade of her shoulder. He peered over her shoulder at the old and new spots her sleeves typically covered. Bruise after bruise welled up in the pattern of a hand not quite her size but still smaller than his own. Most of the small bruises came with a larger mass of purple decorating her skin. "Zinnia, what is the source of those bruises?"

"It is nothing to worry about." She felt her heart stop. Unsure what to do from there, she remained quiet as Islix pulled her arm closer to him to take a closer look.

"Where did they come from?" Islix pressed, but instead, Zinnia slipped out from his arms. She threw back on her apron and ran off, making her way back to the castle, without so much as looking back at him.

Islix wanted to run towards her, to justify his concern. Yet, he did not want to force the reason out of her. He hesitantly stood up from the ground and sheathed his strewn sword, the memory of her bruises

haunting him for the rest of the day and well into the
night.

VII

Islix spent the rest of the afternoon held up in his temporary room within the Royan castle. He knew better than to push onward and look for Zinnia after she had made herself clear that she wanted space. There wasn't much he could do otherwise.

Islix spent the night overthinking, letting the scenes of earlier play out in his head, over and over again. The more he did, the more he felt regret for his actions earlier. He repeated the scenes more times than he could count, wondering where he went wrong. His only question left was the source of the bruises, the answer of which he never quite figured out.

And that left Islix bothered the most. He knew pressing the matter made things worse between them, but otherwise, he felt as though not knowing was somehow more of a nightmare than anything else.

Islix sat at the edge of his bed before deciding to make yet another small drawing, one to focus on the highlight of his day.

His hand moved slowly at first but sped up with extra care in each of his strokes. By the end of the midnight hour, he had a cute scenery created, filled with trees and overgrown flowers surrounding two figures, one towering far over the other, as the two held onto the same massive sword, inspired by his own.

When he straightened his back from his place at his temporary desk, he felt part of it crack, along with the subtle pain building in his shoulders.

Islix took this as his sign to go to sleep.

The next morning came and Islix almost sprinted to his meeting place, beating the other Indomnis, if not all the Royan, to the meeting room. Part of him rushed over in hopes of seeing Zinnia beforehand but as the minutes passed and the room filled, there was no sign of his favorite maid. His newest art piece sat folded up in his pocket, wrapped with a subtle ribbon encircling it.

He let the meeting pass him by, finding himself too tired to fight General Ozburn and his newest line of tangents. He could only hope they would come and go with some sort of speed.

Another day passed by, and the same result.

By the time the third day had come to start, Islix began to be suspicious.

Hour after hour, Islix did his best to make it through the alliance discussions to the halfway point. When he did, his heart pounded away, waiting for the right moment to step away. Aslin seated beside him, having seen Islix and the worry increase with each passing day, decided to take the moment to approach Ozburn on their own volition. The moment gave Islix the chance to sneak out of the meeting room, letting Aslin continue her talks with the other general. He went through the door the maids would go through, but found himself hesitant to go any further.

But not having seen Zinnia even once since she ran away from him left Islix far more worried for her than his own consequences.

Islix put up his long black hair into a bun behind him and snuck around an unknown section of the castle he had never seen before. Down a short, dark hallway, he found a room in which two other maids had been cleaning, both of whom stopped when they heard footsteps. The redhead maid with her hair up in a messy ponytail at the nearest of the entryway looked up at Islix not with fear but with a faint sense of disdain and for a moment, familiarity. The blonde maid looked back down and carried on with her work.

"Hello, I do not mean to intrude but–"

"Are you Islix?" The redhead interrupted, eyeing him warily.

He nodded. "I seek Zinnia, I have not seen her recently and wondered where she could be."

"That's strange," The blonde maid in the corner continued to clean. "I haven't seen her either. Have you, Camellia?"

"Honest, we thought she was...with you." The redhead's face furrowed with worry.

"Has she mentioned me?" Islix felt his cheeks flare with warmth and a small aura of embarrassment.

"She mentioned a massive Indomnis general with horns larger than Ozburn's face. This checks out, right Lillian?" Camellia asked the other, her face stung with worry. She placed her brush down, looking to Islix with suspicion. "But that leaves the question of where Zinnia is."

Islix shared her worry, suddenly not feeling so awful about sneaking away and seeking her out. The bruises on her arms flashed in his memory, his concern growing.

"Have you noticed any markings or bruises on her?" Islix found himself asking the two maids.

Camellia's eyes widened, while Lillian in the corner completely froze from her sweeping.

No one said anything for a moment, the energy in the room shifting.

"Why?" The redhead retorted with pain in her voice.

"I have seen nothing but purple and red lining parts of her arms. Is there someone you suspect that could be–"

"Ozburn." Both women said, their shared disgust permeating in the room.

Islix felt his heart drop, the unfortunate line of swears lining his mind ready to burst out of his mouth.

"Is there any place I should check? Where should I go?"

"You never heard this but us maids are off limits to General Ozburn's room. So, do not go back up the stairs you came from, do not follow that hall, and do not enter the very last room to the left." Camellia said with clear intentions in her stare.

"Do not look closely at the awful portrait there, either." Lillian chimed in.

Islix felt his heart quicken, now more than ever dedicated to finding Zinnia before returning to the meeting. If he would return.

He hurried out of the room, praying Aslin could keep Ozburn's attention for as long as possible.

Islix quickly followed the directions given to him and made his way up to the hall in almost no time. With no guards or soldiers around due to the meeting, he was able to get to the door of General Ozburn's bedroom with no problems.

He went to turn the handle but felt resistance against his hand. Now the only issue left was getting through the locked door in front of him.

Islix looked up and down the hall before taking out one of the long pins from his coat. He carefully used his pin to play with the lock, until the latch finally gave in with a click. He slowly opened the door, peering inside the general's room. When he saw nothing, Islix continued inside, taking in the mess of his desk with curiosity. He approached the large wooden desk filled to the brim with papers, taking a close look at them.

Islix sighed, ready to laugh at himself, at everything this day had brought him. He shook his head, holding his breath.

Ozburn had a lot of explaining to do.

He took the first few papers in hand, folding them before placing them deep in his inner pocket, beside the piece he made and wrapped up for Zinnia.

As he continued to look around the room, a particularly prominent painting of Ozburn graced his presence. Remembering the words of the blonde maid, Islix' face shifted with disgust, touching the gilded gold frame of the painting. The side came out towards him as if on a hinge and he soon discovered a door.

Beyond that door was a short hall, completely unlit, but he braved through it anyways.

At the very end sat a strange, small room, no larger than a broom closet.

There sat Zinnia, eyes closed and propped against the stone wall behind her.

Islix hastily knelt before her, touching her face as she roused from her exhaustion. Her small face leaned into his hand, taking in the warmth against her cold cheeks. Between Islix picking her up and taking her out of the small hall, Zinnia mumbled words he could not hear and fell back into his arms.

Islix made way to his room, taking care not to get caught on his way back.

VIII

Islix left Zinnia on his bed, abandoning talks of alliances after recent discoveries; Ozburn had been abusive to the maids and soldiers around the castle. Of all suspicions, he no longer wondered about the unkempt appearances around the Royan territory. He paced around the room, unsure what to do next.

Honestly, he was beyond lost. A part of him wondered if he could catch the attention of Aslin, but he did not draw any attention to himself in the process.

And if Ozburn gets suspicious, it may not work in their favor.

Islix pondered his options as they stood now; risk Ozburn finding out she's missing and keep Zinnia here. Or take the hour break to make her comfortable, return to the meeting, and get Aslin's help after to form some sort of plan.

Islix sat at the edge of the bed, pulling a blanket over her, and taking her hand into his. He silently inspected the bruises along her arms, thinking of the place he had found her in. Why Ozburn would do such a thing was beyond his comprehension, but his anger rose. Thinking about the reactions of the other soldiers and maids, this painted the idea that these were common occurrences.

Zinnia shifted in the bed, turning around to face him, her heavy eyes settling on him.

Islix held onto her hand, looking from her arm to her face. Concern wouldn't begin to cover half of what he was feeling in that moment.

"Why?" The only word he managed to say, his voice low enough only for her to hear.

Zinnia struggled as she sat up in his bed and shifted herself closer to his side. She looked ready to say something but stayed silent, her eyes downcast to her bruised arms.

"Why were you in there?" Islix asked, fixing the pillow behind her. Zinnia ran her thumb over his hand, surprised at how soft his skin was beneath her hand. But his wary stare refused to lessen, awaiting an answer.

"Underperforming maids are sent to the room as punishment, without food or water. It is Ozburn's way of motivating us to be better. He chooses the duration depending on how he feels. Noticing I had fallen behind in my work, he issued his warnings." Zinnia looked to the bruises lining her arm before rubbing her eyes with her free hand. "When I did not improve, he threw me in soon after."

Islix nodded solemnly, letting the details settle in his mind.

The bruises had already been there the night they spent together under the stars, in the rose garden, and even the day where he let her swing his sword. However long he had been there seemed to align with the marks.

"Why hide this from me? Why not ask for my help when we were alone?"

"My underperforming is my problem, my consequence for my actions."

"That is absurd, Zinnia. No one should be thrown around as a consequence."

"Islix, your chance for peace means more than me." Zinnia said with a sense of finality.

Islix let go of her hand and pulled her chin to face him and only him. The stoic look she knew so well turned fierce.

"I fear no man, dearest Zinnia. Especially one so pathetic, he beats others weaker than himself." Islix leaned in close, the warmth of his breath settling against her flushed cheeks. "I need no alliance with such people. Then, there is you. Willing to go to such lengths for another's peace." His voice dropped even lower, his lips almost brushing against hers.

"I think you deserve to feel safe." Zinnia leaned in to close the leftover gap. The gentle movement was welcome, his hand curving from her chin into her hair, cupping the back of her head. He welcomed the taste of her, though remained careful with her in case she might change her mind.

But Zinnia's lips moved with his, with the same fervor, her delicate hand remaining on the red of his cheek. Her lips moved in tandem with his, happy to accept every part of him with open arms. She lived for every moment she remained in his embrace before he pulled back. His breath heavy, he could not tear away his eyes from the flustered Zinnia that soon settled onto his lap.

Islix felt his heart quake with heat, beating harder than ever.

So much of him wanted to keep going. To show Zinnia other sides of him no other had seen before. But another slowed him down, reminding him of the situation he had just pulled Zinnia from.

Neither of them were safe. Not until Islix could get Zinnia out of the castle. He could barely comprehend the things Ozburn would do to her now that he helped her escape.

Islix took a deep breath, pressing his forehead against hers, and letting his fingers slide through the curls of her hair. His dark eyes watched her carefully, easily sensing her exhaustion. She needed rest more than anything. And he needed a plan now more than ever.

"Can you wait for me here until I return?" Islix's soft voice lingered in the air between them. She nodded, earning a tired smile back. "I will do my best to cut this meeting short. In the meantime, make sure to rest for me." He said, placing her back into his bed. Before he could get up from her side, Zinnia took his hand. The worrisome expression told him everything he needed to know before she spoke up.

"Do not think I will leave you here after this." A serious shift in his expression reflected in his body language, his back straightening up. "I will send someone up briefly, do not be frightened when you hear a knock." Islix finished before leaving the room.

Islix hurried back down to the meeting room, entering as Aslin recited a section of Indomnis history, earning nothing but eye rolls from both groups. Islix snuck back into the meeting room, keeping to the back wall. He placed a hand on the shoulder of one of his soldiers and whispered something in his ear. The soldier nodded frantically, alarm crossing his face before proceeding to leave the room. Islix did the same to the two on his right, telling them to find the maids and escort them back to the Indomnis castle. The next two left the room shortly after, making sure not to look at the opposing general. He moved across the group to the front, watching the lecture with feigned interest.

Aslin knew how to keep a crowd occupied when they needed to, leaving Islix relieved he left them in charge. He didn't dare interrupt, letting them naturally finish their lecture some moments later.

"Aslin, I am honored to have witnessed one of your lectures of our history. Have you told our future allies of the most recent triumph in battle?" Islix urged them on, hoping to buy some time for his soldiers to work without intrusion. He seated himself, feeling Ozburn's eyes burn into him for the mere suggestion of more history.

This should buy just a little bit more time, he thought.

After the good part of an hour, Islix motioned for Aslin to finish up and stood in their place. As they passed one another, he gave Aslin a small note in hand. He towered over his friend as they took his seat and he made way to the middle of both groups.

"We the Indomnis have a sense of pride in everything we do, as Aslin described. Though within that pride, we know to keep an open mind, for there are some things we do not look past without a thorough time of introspection." Islix said, looking at Ozburn, who watched curiously. "I believe we need some time to fully analyze if an alliance is necessary between the Indomnis and the Royan. With that being said, I want to thank you personally, General Ozburn, for housing us in leu of these discussions. But as of now, we will be leaving today to make the walk back to our home." He said with a solemn expression, leading off his soldiers out of the room without so much as a second look at the opposing general.

Islix went back to his temporary room and slowly opened the door, revealing Zinnia upright in his bed. Her eyes lit up upon seeing him in the doorway. She looked far better than before, having sent one of his soldiers to bring food and water to the room. Now he had a small opening of time to retreat with Zinnia back to his own castle, looking forward now more than ever to be home.

He sat at her bedside, feeling her cheek with the back of his hand. "Have you eaten enough?" Islix asked, inspecting the rest of her as she nodded. "Good.

I know it is short notice, but we must leave immediately."

"What?" She looked up at him, feeling his hand curve around her cheek.

"I told you, I would rather not leave you here. Not with Ozburn." His hand enveloped the back of her head, his choice set in stone.

"What if you regret taking me with you?" Zinnia mumbled. But Islix only smiled at her question.

"I have no regrets, Zinnia. I am one who follows their first heart and has yet to regret that so far." He said, helping Zinnia stand up by keeping her steady. His hands held her lower back, not letting go until he was confident she could stand.

"You and I shall be taking our leave from the garden. I noticed a place by the wall you took me to near the rose garden, but we will need to be careful getting there. Are you ready?" Islix asked softly, not wanting to let go of her hand. He felt her squeeze his hand as he slowly led her to the door.

Zinnia nodded, confident in her stance. Islix squeezed her hand back and led the two out into the empty hall, left to carefully wander the castle until they found the courtyard.

IX

The sun peaked above them, but the incoming clouds took away the warmth of the sun. The two of them wandered off into the Royan castle courtyard, its overgrown state allowing them the cover they needed. As they reached the small bundles of roses by the crumbled wall, Islix was given confirmation he was on the right track. The supposed straight path back to the Indomnis border, with Zinnia constantly finding herself staring at something new every so often. As worried as he was, Islix indulged her curiosity when he could, but eventually emphasized their need to hurry.

Islix's worries rested on whether Ozburn would discover her disappearance before the two of them could make it back safely. He was unsure he could fight off one of the generals and keep Zinnia safe at the same time. He felt a rising sense of paranoia, his eyes constantly keeping to a rhythm of scanning the surrounding area of the open road every so often. At one point, even the scatter of leaves could raise his heartrate. While he never spotted anyone, he always remained alert, refusing to be caught off guard.

Islix soon saw the Indomnis castle coming into view, the four towers he knew so well alleviating the anxiety of their walk back home. They rose far above the castle he called home, edging close to the barely visible clouds in the sky.

Relief washed over him as soon as he was met with familiar faces at his front gates. Though he was quick to settle in for the incoming evening, he was uncertain how Zinnia beside him would take to an entirely new place. As he put Zinnia back down, her exhausted eyes barely took the time to register an entire new castle. The stonework had little gaps in between them, the floor smooth and even, every sconce decorated with barely burnt candles. While the two walked side by side, no words exchanged between them, even as they stood alone in the middle of the castle's largest hallway.

Regardless of where the two of them were, Zinnia was still in danger. He made the decision to keep her in the room besides his own, hoping for her understanding. The two stood before the door to her new room in silence, the gentle rays of the setting sun dissolving throughout the large hallway. He looked to the human beside him, wondering what he could say after everything the two of them went through today.

"Are you okay?" Islix asked, voice soft as he inspected the questioning look on her face. She nodded, her eyes remaining on the door, unknowingly taking a deep breath before releasing it back out.

"I haven't left the castle in years. Before that, I don't think I have ever even left town. My nerves are showing, aren't they?" She touched her suddenly warm face, struggling to shake off her anxiety.

"It may not be much to comfort, but know this," He ran his hand softly through her hair. "My home is yours." Islix finished.

Zinnia smiled, entering her new room with him behind her.

The area was spacious, a newly made bed, and open windows that invited the much needed warmth into her room. Simple as it was, she looked beyond ecstatic, until her face dropped soon after.

"Is it too small?" Islix asked, worried and partly embarrassed.

"No, I love it, I really do." She said, but turned to him with a short look of unease. "Is it strange of me to worry over the others back at the castle?"

Islix pulled Zinnia into him, wrapping his arms around her back, resting his chin on the top of her head.

It was moments like these that he found her so endearing.

"I will do my best to ease these worries, Zinnia." He said, feeling her hands tenderly rest on his sides. "Ozburn will not get away with any of this."

"Do you have a plan I don't know about?" She chuckled, his arms tightening.

"Perhaps. But you need not think about that. It is my job to worry, not yours." He pulled back to look at her, feeling her pull away completely to sit on the edge of the bed.

"What if I cannot help but worry?" Zinnia placed her hands on her lap, playing with a loose thread of her wrinkled uniform. Islix didn't hesitate to sit next to her.

"Then I suppose two of us are like minded in that way."

"I guess so." Zinnia bumped her shoulder into his, her disdain remaining on her face.

"I am always ready to listen, if you need it. A lot has happened to you in a short span of time."

Zinnia thought for a moment, the thoughtful look in her face compiling the last few days worth of drama and hell.

In the last couple of weeks, she had been thrown around, yelled at, tossed into the worst punishment for those underperforming, been rescued, and now she was in a completely different place, away from her only friends who were now more in danger than ever before.

So, it made sense to her when she started feeling the sting of warm tears come down her cheeks.

"I'm afraid for the others, Islix. Whether Ozburn shows up here, or stays there, it feels as though someone gets hurt in the process. It is juvenile, but I worry for the people on both sides." Zinnia felt Islix's hand on her face, swiping away tears with his thumb. "Would it be strange to ask you if there is any way I can help? It might put my mind at ease."

Islix kissed her cheek, making sure to settle an arm around her back once more before speaking.

"I had ordered some of my soldiers to escort the other maids who told me where you may have been. It seemed only right to avoid them sharing the same fate as you."

"Really? Are Camellia and Lilian here already?" Her eyes lit up as she frantically wiped away her remaining tears from her cheek with her sleeve.

He nodded, relieved to see her smile again.

His worry for her remained, not having fully processed the fact that she had been thrown into a barren room with nothing in it, to starve and dehydrate, as a means of punishment.

But for now, Islix settled back his anger, pushing it back for another day, another time.

Islix went to leave, but felt Zinnia's hand settle in his as she stopped him. When he turned to ask her why, she didn't give him the chance to speak up before the words left her mouth, "Can we go see them?"

He nodded and led the two out into the hallway and into the main room. Zinnia let go of his hand, his warmth leaving him and going with her as she practically tackled the two maids who hugged her back, the Indomnis soldiers beside them making space for their reunion.

Zinnia felt a small wave of relief wash over her, not noticing anything out or the ordinary on her friends as she looked them both up and down. Camellia took Zinnia's wrist into her hand, investigating the marks left on her. Lillian slid back Zinnia's sleeve even further, revealing far more severe bruising until the seam at her elbow.

Before he could approach the group of women, Islix felt a familiar hand on his shoulder, turning to see Aslin. He let out a breath of relief, but the look in their face was not shared.

"Islix," Aslin said under her breath, letting a couple of Indomnis soldiers pass by them before continuing. "We need to talk. I have intel on Ozburn through one of the Royan soldiers. I may have figured out why he wanted an alliance."

"Then we may have learned the same thing." Islix said, tapping his chest pocket, full of stolen papers from Ozburn's room. "But let us save it for later. I think everyone needs a break, if not just for the night."

Aslin hesitated, but once they felt the sore exhaustion of coming back home catch up with them, they nodded. "Agreed."

Islix let everyone take the remainder of the day for resting, leaving the problems of the Royan for another day, while he let his heart rest on the much more relaxed Zinnia.

The night approached quickly, and Islix put through his arrangements for the currently displaced friends of Zinnia, checked on the soldiers returning from the Royan castle to make sure each were okay, and retreated back to his room to collapse on his bed, letting the exhaustion of today's events wash over him.

By the time everything was said and done, it was at least half past midnight.

Islix groaned, lacking enough energy to undress. He could barely pick his head up from his pillow again, his horns digging into the soft bed beneath him. He unclasped his hair, letting it fall over both sides of him before forcing himself up. He got out of the bed, threw off everything onto a nearby chair except his underwear, and laid back into his bed, letting the darkness of the room overtake him.

Exhausted as he was, sleep did not find him.

A light knock at his door perked up his anxiety, enough that he felt his heart pound when he went to open the door.

Zinnia stood in front of him in simple bed clothes, freshly bathed, with an anxious look crossed on her gentle features. She found herself staring at his loose hair falling over his bare red shoulders and chest, forcefully tearing her eyes away and praying the few seconds she stared went unnoticed. "I keep trying to sleep but when I do, I keep thinking I'm in Ozburn's room again. I am not sure what to do and I'm scared, I was hoping you might still be up." She yawned.

Islix went from exhaustion to a look of unfiltered anger before composing himself. He took her hand and led her inside, closing the door behind her.

"I didn't realize I would think about it so much." She said, barely able to see in his dark room. All she could make out was Islix's full form in front of her, leading her over to his bed.

She felt him guide her to his side to lay down, accompanied with the warmth of his body heat flush against her own before a blanket was pulled over the two of them. His arms wrapped around her waist and onto her back, his face gentle on her shoulder. She felt him exhale heavily, releasing a warm breath along with it.

"I should have run after you that day. I am sorry I let this go on for as long as I did." Islix's voice wallowed with regret. "The moment I let you walk away, I knew I would regret it." His warm breath glided on her shoulder.

"Islix, you did nothing wrong–"

"I promise you this, Zinnia; if Ozburn tries to touch you again, I will kill him where he stands." Islix said, placing a hand on her back, letting his hand find its way up to the back of her neck. He felt her sink further into his chest, her small form settling against his unusual warmth.

"I could not imagine giving you up." He tightened his arms around her, feeling her chest release a long breath.

Unwilling to let her go, Islix and Zinnia found sleep much faster together than they would have alone.

X

The next morning, Islix struggled to leave Zinnia by herself. Knowing her worry over Ozburn and the awful acts committed against her, Islix wanted nothing more than to reiterate his vow to keep her safe. His arms remained around her small form, letting her sleep in through much of the morning in his bed.

The next time Islix woke, his heart was pounding, as if he had awoken from a nightmare. Adrenaline seeped through his veins, bringing with it a need rival to none. Only reminiscent of what he felt when he and Zinnia had been alone in the woods within the Royan castle gardens. When he held her in his lap, there was nothing else he could have wanted in that moment. The feeling of her writhing against his hands, moaning his name, begging for Islix to keep going. The mere thought was enough to leave his cock twitching in his pants.

Zinnia shifted in her sleep, nesting further into the inviting warmth of his chest. Islix kissed the top of her head, willing himself some form of control over his urges.

Islix felt a sudden possessive feeling in his chest, prompting him to keep his arms tight around her. A sensation he had not once felt in his life, but one reigniting his need to protect her.

So long as he could help it, Islix wouldn't let anyone take away their peace.

By the time she had finally roused, Zinnia woke up on Islix, his sleeping form all too new to her. It wasn't often she could catch a glimpse of him in a vulnerable state, giving her all the more reason to let him sleep in. Unfortunately for her, he woke up not too long after, peering out at the distant, low bearing sun.

"Did I wake you up?" She kept her eyes closed, too comfortable to move away from his immense warmth.

"No, I've been awake for a time already." Islix yawned, tentatively rubbing her back. "To think you slept through much of the day. Seems you needed more rest than I thought." He pulled her close, refusing to relinquish any space between them, if not for a bit longer.

As the two eventually got up and dressed for the remaining night, Islix kept Zinnia at his side as much as he could, unable to keep her away for more than a few brief moments without some semblance of worry striking him.

When speaking with Aslin later on in the night, he stressed the idea of taking some time off before confronting the issue of the Royan army and the general whose true intentions were coming to light.

For now, all Islix could do was bide his time.

On her second full day in the Indomnis castle, Zinnia had been taken to get new clothes fitted. Apparently wearing her maid uniform made the other soldiers uncomfortable, with them seeing the Royan colors in their own home. Afterward, Islix struggled to keep himself away for very long, soon taking it upon himself to take Zinnia out into the courtyard and teach her how to properly wield a sword. He made sure to suppress his thoughts before showing her a proper stance. Though after a few scares, he withdrew the idea before she could take off one of their hands.

On the third day, clouds bore low over the castle, leaving the two of them indoors for the day. Islix found himself struggling to leave Zinnia by herself. But he was quickly left with no other choice, going through a cluster of short lived meetings throughout the day.

Then came the fourth day, one where Zinnia did not see Islix leave his room once. Regardless of his presence, she took it upon herself to wander around the castle, getting to know her new surroundings, and treating it as though it were a day trip. She met with her other friends for part of the day, listening to their time in the castle thus far as they walked together. Camellia was distracted as she spoke, while Lillian told Zinnia how she would sneak off into the gardens and take into account all their plants. While Zinnia wanted to scold her, she thought it might encourage her instead, so she held back her comments.

Night came around the corner and she walked past his door again, finding her curiosity rising each time.

Zinnia stopped at the door, inching closer to it before eventually knocking. The door opened almost immediately, putting her face to face with a very unkempt, half-dressed Islix, as if he had just woken up from a nap.

"Are you okay?" Zinnia reached out to smooth out some of his hair from his face and shoulder. She felt his hand instantly grab hers and pull her into the room, slamming the door shut behind her.

The cold door sat flat against her back, and the heat of Islix's bare chest against her body pushed her further into it. His lips lingered against her neck, leaving a bare touch of a kiss to her collarbone. Just as quickly, he forced himself away and let her go. He walked back over to his bed, collapsing beside an empty bottle, with one half full beside him on the floor, the mere light of the various votive candles at his desk revealing his disheveled state.

"Please tell me you haven't been drinking here all day?" Zinnia said, straightening herself out as she actively ignored his odd behavior, and approaching the bed to sit beside his sprawled out form.

He lifted his head to look at her, his eyes looking her up and down, drinking in her form.

"I started only after sunset." He flopped back face down.

"Did something happen?" She pet his hair, smoothing out the back from knots with her nails. "I've been worrying about you all day, Islix. You haven't left the room once."

"I needed some time to think." He sighed. "Please, keep doing that." He openly moaned, the brush of her hands in his hair mixed with the occasional stroke of his horns left him flushed while he lacked a proper filter. She removed her hand and crossed her arms, watching him look up at her scowl.

"Tell me what's wrong." Zinnia insisted. Islix groaned, flipped himself upward, staring at the high ceiling of his room. He looked at her lap, the spot looking far more inviting than anything else. When she settled fully onto his bed and let him lay his head on her, Islix felt a smile grow on his face, until it dropped off of him soon after.

"I read the paperwork I had stolen from Ozburn's office, after putting it off since we came back. Aslin was right, he never wanted an alliance. Had I not fallen in love, gone looking for you, I wouldn't have been in his room, I wouldn't have seen these papers. Everything was a trap."

Zinnia's face flushed with warmth, only a brief nod leaving her.

"Was I truly so blind to him? I sit and wonder if I missed anything else. The first thing I could recall that had me questioning his motives were the looks in the eyes of the soldiers. They seemed so...frightened by him. That is not how a leader should act. Fear is no more a proper tactic than a child having a tantrum." Islix sighed, looking up at Zinnia's concerned face. "It is nothing I cannot handle, no need to look so nervous." He placed an arm over his eyes and shifted in bed.

"It isn't that," Zinnia tried to come up with an excuse, unsure how to mention his comment on 'falling for her' but found a new subject to leave her mouth. "I just worry about you, as I said before, that is all." Her hand reached over his hair, pushing it back from his unusually warm face. Another moan left his mouth as her hand purposefully found the base of his horns.

"Zinnia," His deep voice grumbled against his arm as her nails glided over his scalp. The feeling had him forget the weight of the topic at hand. "Why did you come to find me tonight?" He breathed heavily.

"I was worried about you. Why?" She asked softly, moving her hands up and down the base of his horns with a sense of care.

"Worry for me is wasted." He sighed, a hand lingering on her thigh beneath him.

"Is it so awful to worry?" She asked. "I like being near you."

"Zinnia." His voice deepened. "Zinnia." He barely breathed, struggling to compose himself as she did something as simple as caress his horns.

"Do you want me to stop, Islix?" Her voice came out a bare whisper.

"Never." He hissed back, loving the way she said his name. "Never stop touching me."

Islix felt the tightening of his pants, wanting to give in to his temptation of tearing them off and finishing himself off right then and there in front of her. But embarrassment mixed with his drunken stupor and sensitivity. All he could do was sit there in her lap, one of her hands gently playing with his hair while the other palmed the base of his horns with more than enough pressure. He couldn't stop the moan that left his lips as scattered swears and ragged panting left him, his hips gently bucking beneath her touch.

Islix felt the wet warmth pool between his thighs, struggling to catch his breath. His hand remained tight on her thigh but lessened once he realized what he had done. Horrified with himself, he removed his arm to meet her startled honey eyes, which stared down at him with red across both cheeks.

"Are you okay?" Zinnia's soft voice whispered in his ear, relief mixing with terror in his chest.

"Yes," Islix prayed she did not notice. Perhaps it wasn't so obvious what occurred. "I think I may have had too much to drink."

"After watching that, I have to agree." She smiled, wiping back some of the sweat from his forehead. Islix stopped breathing for a moment after fully registering the comment.

Perhaps she did notice.

Zinnia and Islix shared a look with one another before she shifted his head off her lap.

Islix grabbed her hand into his, tightening it to keep her from leaving the bed.

"Zinnia," His low voice remained out of breath. She froze at the sound of her name, a bit too stunned to leave. Islix sat upright, moving close to her, enough that his chest pushed against her.

Zinnia pressed a single hand to his bare chest, feeling the quick beat of his heart beneath her touch. She ran another one up to his cheek, feeling the warmth of his face against her cold skin. She held it carefully, her uncertain eyes drifting up to him.

"I think you need rest, Islix." She said with a gentle whisper. She left a brief kiss to his cheek as she slid out of his bed and quickly out of his room.

Islix fell over onto the bed, wondering what had gone through his head to lose himself while she touched him. He replayed the scene in his head, recalling more the feeling of her hands on his horns, and the way she made him writhe under her touch until sleep found him once again.

XI

Life in the Indomnis castle was unlike anything Zinnia had ever experienced.

Zinnia struggled to find sleep, the sound of Islix spilling his feelings as if breathing another breath taking up so much of her mind, among the other parts of her night. Her thoughts settled on the scene, replaying his words over and over again.

As long as she had been alive, never did Zinnia think life would change in the span of a couple weeks, leaving behind the castle she worked for her entire life. The last year or so were far more severe than others, but she still felt a complex nostalgia for what she once knew.

Since the day of her fourteenth birthday, Zinnia worked as a maid at the same castle for a little over a decade, measuring her every minute by what needed to be tidied, scrubbed, or otherwise cleaned. Never having a real day off outside of illness, she managed to make a life for herself there, regardless of her status as a maid.

During her first year of her maid service, she managed to befriend others within her job, many of which would come and go throughout the years. The only two to stick around with almost identical tenure being Camellia and Lillian, two of the most starkly opposite souls she had ever met. Regardless, she would call them her sisters in a heartbeat, closer to her than her own family.

Camellia had been there since before Zinnia's arrival, but Lillian only came five years prior. The amount of times Camellia would cover for her clumsy mistakes, it was no surprise the two of them grew so close over the years.

Zinnia had never heard Camellia delve into her past, nor much of anything about herself. However, the two of them would share one strange common ground no other maid would ever share with them; their shared love for war strategy and weaponry. In the rare moments that the two of them could sneak away from their jobs, Camellia and Zinnia would spend time in the armory. While Zinnia's nerves would always get the best of her and keep her from picking up any swords or otherwise, she had no issue watching Camellia practice, filling the empty space between with whatever she had overheard that week.

In rare moments that Lillian would come to join them, the youngest of the maids would seldom speak of herself, always talking about some book she had found in her latest scouting of the Royan castle library. She had a love for novels and tales of adventures unlike anything else. Lillian frequently opted to sneak away to the library whenever a moment came free. Understanding, both Camellia and Zinnia respected her space, but always made it a point to invite her, even if she brought a book with her. It was always made clear if she wanted company, but to be left alone as well, both were plausible.

Zinnia threw a pillow over her eyes, thinking of all the changes that came in the blink of an eye. She could only wonder if these changes would bring the three of them peace, or more problems than it was worth.

It wasn't until an hour or so later that she was able to fall asleep.

The next day came as though the night before didn't happen. Zinnia retreated from bed, dressing in the new clothes fitted for her recently. She picked out a long black skirt with the sides longer than the front, a matching crimson shirt with lace sleeves stopping at her wrist, and brushed out her curls before putting them up with ribbon, leaving the room in a hurry.

Zinnia wandered around the castle as she would in the morning, taking part of her day to catch up with Camellia and Lillian in the library, a place the women accepted as their regular meeting spot. The other two wore similar outfits, the same red to accent their clothing in one way or another. For Camellia, her skirt had a loose crimson belt adoring her waist, while Lillian wore a short-sleeve version of Zinnia's blouse.

Conversations flowed freely, without the worry of having to return to work or whispering so General Ozburn would not overhear them. While Lillian took control of the conversation, citing the last of the Royan castles novels she had taken with her, Camellia remained as secretive as ever, only nodding or shaking her head, with rare moments of her ever speaking up.

To Zinnia's surprise, she noticed Aslin walk past the library almost three times in the last hour. As Lillian went on about her adjustment to no longer working, Camellia stared out the hallway, brow furrowed which told Zinnia she noticed, and now, seemingly waited for Aslin to walk by again.

As if on cue, Aslin walked past and peered inside briefly, meeting Camellia's harsh glare with their own.

"Is everything okay, did I miss something?" Zinnia asked under her breath, with Lillian nowhere near stopping her current tale.

Camellia shot a glare back at Zinnia, quickly forcing her to retract her statement. The remainder of the morning was spent listening to Lillian prattle about her latest finding in the Indomnis castle.

Zinnia wasn't sure what to do about the rest of her day, finding herself trying to avoid Islix and his room. So, she did the first thing she was invited to, and spent the remainder of her day with Lillian, walking around the expanse of the Indomnis castle garden together.

Lillian had made it a point to come out here every day, strolling through the flowers every chance she could. As the two of them walked together, Zinnia couldn't help but notice fresh soil along one of the paths further away from the castle, fully bloomed white lily flowers beside much of their stroll back towards the entrance to the castle.

"Isn't this amazing?" Lillian commented, her green eyes drinking in the gentle view of the gardens. With every step, the two of them could tell someone took their job seriously. Perfectly cared for, each section led by low grass, nowhere near the height of their knees as it was at the Royan castle. The two began in the very front of the courtyard, taking in the round topiaries at the edge of the outer walls. The path led them down into a line of multicolored roses, all in the boldest shade of red.

"Makes you wonder, doesn't it?" Zinnia asked, her steps slow as she took in the beauty around them.

"Hm?" Lillian barely paid attention, her sight set on the next section of flowers in front of them.

"Do you think the garden in the Royan castle had ever looked like this before General Ozburn took charge?"

"Camellia once told me they did. Once upon a time." Lillian's face dropped, her steps hurrying forward. "Never mind that, come see this, Zinnia!" Her voice hollered from afar, forcing Zinnia to move faster. She could not match the speed of her friend, but pushed herself regardless, not wanting to get left behind in a courtyard she barely knew how to maneuver through. When she finally caught up to Lillian, her friend's abrupt halt almost had Zinnia smacking right into her back.

But the walk had been well worth it.

Both Zinnia and Lillian laid their eyes on bushes of pink peonies, their pink color bold against the dark trunks of the trees behind them, all lined perfectly next to one another.

Whoever took care of this grand display of a courtyard took their job very seriously.

On their way back, all Zinnia could think of was how perfect the gardens were, especially compared to what she had seen before. She no longer wondered why Lillian would spend much of her time outside, after all, who wouldn't want to be surrounded by flowers all day?

As day turned into night once more, she stopped by the library before she escaped back into her room, holding the stack with her arm and chin up top to secure it from toppling over. She let the pile of books drop onto the nearby desk, trying to decide which one to break into first. Zinnia picked up a few on the history of archery, a skill she wished to hone now that she was free of duty. She always wanted to learn how to use some sort of weapon in case she would ever need it, recalling her sessions with Islix and his sword with a small blush while reading.

She took a moment to wonder if Lillian would lend her some of the books she had taken with her from the Royan castle library. Her heart beat happily with the idea of being able to read in peace for once, before her thoughts trailed back to Ozburn. She truly wondered if the man had ever stepped in there deliberately.

Then again, with the sheer number of books in Lillian's possession, perhaps not.

While she drifted back into reading, hour after hour passed without interruption, until an eventual light knock on her door left her hesitant to answer.

Yet, Zinnia found herself at the door faster than she cared to admit.

XII

"Zinnia?" Islix's voice sounded out, muffled but distinct, even with the door between them.

Zinnia huffed, not ready by any means but hesitantly let the door open.

Islix walked into the room, wearing his typical leather armor and his hair up, bearing a bottle of alcohol in one hand and flowers in the other.

She sighed, begrudgingly shutting the door behind him. "What is all this for?" Zinnia asked, returning to the edge of her bed.

He popped open the cork to the bottle and handed it off to her, his expression solemn and careful. The drink's sweet scent was heavily reminiscent of last night.

"We drink to discuss." He urged.

She watched him carefully, before taking her first swig of the drink, its sweet taste dissolving on its way down her throat. She handed off the bottle to him as he sat beside her, drinking far more than the single sip she took.

"Are you angry at me for last night?" Islix spoke his thoughts aloud.

"No, I'm not angry so to speak." She said matter-of-factly. "I guess I'm surprised that you decided to tell me you 'fell for me' so indirectly. It has me wondering if you're embarrassed by me."

Islix fell silent this time, thinking back to last night as best he could. But besides embarrassing himself as she touched him, he barely recalled the words coming out of himself.

Not that he didn't mean every single of them.

"I see." Islix said, putting the bottle down on the desk beside them. "I thought you were upset at me for a...different reason."

"I knew what touching you had been doing. It was a choice I made." She said, reaching over him for the bottle. She took another hefty sip of the drink before placing it back down, held steady between her thighs. "I'm sorry if anything."

Islix let her words settle in his mind. He certainly didn't expect her to say she chose to touch him, aware of what happened when she did so.

"For what?" He looked directly at her for the first time since he was allowed into the room.

"For not stopping, I should have known better. For letting myself get upset at all. Both of those things."

Islix took her chin into his hand, making sure her honey eyes were on him. "I should have been more honest, more direct. About how much I enjoy your company, how I have thought about you every day since we met. I wonder why your eyes lingered on me in that meeting hall, if the smile you sent my way that day had been solely for me, or if you smile at others that way. But I never once saw that look on your face for anyone else. I still struggle to understand why you would put yourself at risk for the Indomnis, for peace that was never meant to be. For me, a stranger in your home." He leaned in, brushing his lips against hers, moving the bottle away. "I sit and wonder what I could have done to deserve such a strong being to be in my presence."

"Islix." Zinnia's vision quivered, tears lining her eyes.

"I love hearing you say my name. How sweet it sounds coming from you." He kissed her cheek, his hand encompassing the other side of her face and part of her hair. He worked his way down to her neck, gentle with her collarbone. "I only wish I could have been more in control of myself last night. My plan was to ask you to share a bed with me again, and all I did was ruin everything." He muttered against her skin. Part of him began to lack the patience to play this back and forth game with her, wanting her to touch him again, more than just his horns.

"There is always tonight." She said, her voice small against his.

"There is indeed always tonight." He repeated, a light sigh settling against her neck.

Islix smiled before he bit into her collarbone. He towered over her small form, his lips roaming every part of her body he could get to as he pulled her with him onto the bed, barely hovering above her. He felt her hands settle on his back before making their way up to his horns again. The subtle touch sent shivers down his back, his lips returning to hers with a fervor unlike anything else. She felt his tongue dart between her lips before tasting every part of her he could get.

Zinnia's hand made it to the back of his head, playing with his hair as she did the night before. Islix felt her hand run through his hair, scratching lightly against his scalp. The feeling had him gently moan, melting into her every touch. He held her waist with one hand while the other made a fist above her, grabbing the pillow as if it was a way to maintain what control of himself he had left. When he playfully bit her lower lip, the sweetest noise came out of her, leaving him overheating in the bed. The feeling of her against his body, touching him so carefully that Islix was unable to form a coherent thought.

"Zinnia." His deep voice rumbled against her lips. "Do not rouse what you cannot tame."

But her hands remained, her heart beating in a quick unity with his. His knee remained between her legs, separating her thighs, his teeth biting down on her lower lip, a short rumble of a moan leaving his throat.

Islix wanted to tear at the clothes on her body, rip off fabric wherever his hands could reach. But he wanted to bare himself as he was to her, show her everything he was before they could continue. He carefully unclasped his shirt and let it lay open, her hands careful as they glided over every open part of his chest. She carefully touched every part of him, letting herself take in the shape of his body. Every line, every marking, all part of a story on his timeline.

Her honey eyes blinked, the light of the candles illuminating the faded red that colored his skin. Islix sat calmly, letting her take her time. He felt the pull of his pants lower from his hips, slowly exposing him to the night air. Before she could continue, Islix placed a hand over hers.

"Zinnia, none of this is needed if you do not wish it, I am perfectly fine with simply sharing a space together and nothing more." He sighed heavily, trying to catch his breath. But her hands continued, watching him carefully as she pulled off the rest of his clothing. Islix felt her hands settle on his bare hips, sliding to his lower back.

"What if I like hearing you say my name?" She whispered back, feeling his hand tighten on her waist, enough pressure to leave a mark if he kept holding on. His other hand moved to her face, cupping her cheek before stealing her lips once more, another groan rumbling in his throat. Before he knew it, he was lifting her shirt, careful in how he took off her clothes, fighting back how much he wanted to rip everything off.

When bared to him, Islix still found himself staring more at her honey eyes than any other part of her.

Awaiting and patient, as she always was.

"Zinnia." Islix smiled, her name leaving his lips in a deep exhale. Her face, normally a pale complexion, held more color to them now than he had ever seen. His hand withdrew from her face, sliding down to her breasts, over her belly, and soon to her entrance. He dragged a finger over her slick folds, feeling the warmth of her settle around him as he gently placed a finger of her.

The awaiting look in her honey eyes was replaced with a heavy-lidded gaze, one that watched him carefully as he let his fingertips trace every part inside of her. Her unsteady breath lingered in the air between them, her need rising with every touch. Zinnia felt her heart beat quicker with every stroke, prompting her to reach out for his horns. The feral noise that left him had forced his hand to retreat, replacing it with his cock in a matter of seconds.

Islix settled himself inside of her, slow as he pushed as deep as he could, holding back his need to feel all of her warmth surrounding him. Control became difficult, the feeling of her hands palming at the base of his horns. He slid into her as far as he could, letting the fog of lust overtake him as his slow thrusts quickened. He pushed into her, over and over, both hands holding onto her hips to keep her in place.

Zinnia's soft moans gave way to a loud cry of need, and soon after, his name left her mouth as softly as the day they met. As a needy noise left her lips, a new warmth flooded him, the last of his control leaving his body.

Islix was nowhere near as subtle, a growl of her name leaving his lips as he released himself in her, thrusting until his hips could no longer bear it.

The needy look in her eyes replaced with exhaustion, Zinnia breathed heavily, reaching out to smooth back Islix's hair from his sweaty forehead. He took her hand away, bringing it up to his lips instead.

Zinnia pulled him down to her, hand tangled in his hair, leaving kiss after kiss along the side of his face, before ending back to his lips where she began.

XIII

Zinnia awoke the next day wrapped up in Islix's arms, his chest becoming her pillow. She settled further into him, feeling his arms tighten around her. The early morning light coming through her window forced her to retreat her face into him. A brief chuckle rumbled through him, one hand settling on the back of her hair while the other held tight around her back.

"Darling, I can do most things, but I cannot make the light go away." Islix muttered into her ear, holding her as if to protect her from the sunlight.

She simply grumbled once more before a frantic knock at her door took them both away from their dreamy state.

Islix and Zinnia looked at the door, wondering who on earth could be awake at such an ungodly hour.

"Islix? I know you're in there." Aslin's intense voice sounded through the door. Islix quickly put on his clothes as Zinnia sank into the bed, both out of embarrassment and exhaustion.

Islix opened the door, absolutely disheveled but the dreamlike state on his face was enough to leave Aslin shaking their head.

"Say it isn't so, this was me taking a wild guess by the way." They pushed back their short tight curls away from their horns, their typically relaxed face now tense with worry. "General Ozburn is at our gates, demanding to meet with you."

"Are you serious?" Islix asked, Zinnia perking up from the bed in horror.

"I have been in your leadership for a decade, and not once have I ever found it upon myself to lie to you." They said, inhaling a deep breath. "I beg that you have a plan before coming out. But if I may suggest one thing; we need to keep the Royan women hidden and away from him. Just in case." Aslin said, already having thought about the possibilities. She forced back her nerves, putting her most confident, stoic face for not just Islix but for herself and her soldiers.

Islix smoothed back his hair, finding himself solemn in his thoughts. He agreed, telling Aslin that Ozburn is not to be left alone. They nodded, back straightening as they tried to push back the worry creasing their face.

When he shut the door, Islix shared a felled look with Zinnia, watching her carefully.

"Zinnia, I need you to do something for me. Take Camellia and Lillian and go to the courtyard with Aslin. Do not come back for any reason, I will be the one to come get you. Do you understand me?" Islix spoke with a sense of dread, forcing Zinnia's hesitant nod.

"Good." He said, looking at his coat and recalling the papers held within it. Before fully dressing, he took Zinnia's face into his hands, kissing her deeply as if it would be his last. "Please take this as well." He took one of the sheathed knives from his pocket, handing it to Zinnia, and wrapping his hand over hers. His black eyes took in her concerned expression, looking over every part of her face. "If you find yourself endangered, use it if you need it."

"Islix, what do I do if–"

"Do not fight me, I said I would come back for you. Please, take my word." He said, kissing her cheek before retreating towards the door. He looked back at her, his gentle smile no longer visible. "Twenty minutes, and I need the three of you in the courtyard. Not a minute more."

She frantically nodded, steeling herself for what was to come.

Zinnia rushed from her room, dressed in the same skirt and blouse from the day before, frantically knocking on Camellia's door. It wasn't long before she emerged fully dressed, a stressful angry look scrawled across her expression that begged to be asked how and why she was already prepared. But before any words could leave her, Zinnia was dragged off by Camellia and the two ran towards Lillian's room, forcing her to get dressed and leave with them. She refused to leave with them until she could grab a book to bring along with her, leaving Zinnia a bit frustrated, but earning a strange understanding from Camellia.

The three hurried off down the hall towards the gardens, finding themselves with a few other Indomnis soldiers, including an awaiting Aslin.

"Good morning, ladies. I apologize for disturbing all of you, but it is only temporary." Aslin said to all them, avoiding staring at one for too long.

"Temporary, but the real problems sit inside." Camellia crossed her arms, the angry look in her eyes piercing back at Aslin. "We'll be back at Royan castle by nightfall, I can already tell." She commented, disgust lining her expression.

"Please understand one thing, Camellia," Aslin stared back, an almost knowing look in her pitch black eyes. "Islix would never agree to such a thing." She retorted.

"Yeah, I place all my trust in a man I've known for a week," Camellia shot back. "Ozburn can't be trusted, nor do you seem to know what he is capable of."

"You are correct, I don't know anything about Ozburn besides what he has been plotting. However, I do know the man speaking with him. And I trust my leader with my life." She said, a short draw of breath leaving her lungs.

Camellia scowled, letting the last word go to her, while the others remained silent with worry.

Zinnia felt her fear diminish with Aslin's words. She soon realized that she wanted to fight for her freedom as much as Islix had been doing on her and the other women's behalf. He could have easily taken her and left the others behind. But here all three were, with a guard Islix trusted more than anyone else.

In a split second decision, Zinnia knew there was an easier way to get General Ozburn to leave.

It just required some rule breaking.

Lillian struggled to keep still, prompting Aslin to try and talk with her, an attempt to keep her mind occupied. As Zinnia stood closest to the door back into the castle, her vision darted carefully between

Aslin, taken by conversation with Lillian, and the same door they entered from.

Islix sat across General Ozburn in the much smaller meeting hall of the Indomnis castle. His arms crossed, chin elevated, and a concerning stare at the older man nothing less than obvious.

"What are you doing here, Ozburn?" Islix asked, forcing himself to focus on the man across from him, against the fleeting thoughts of Zinnia and the safety of the others.

"I think you already understand why I am here." Ozburn said, staring back at Islix with deprecation. "Why have you taken my maids away?"

"Before you ask anything, I have questions of my own." Islix narrowed his eyes, willing himself to maintain his calm nature. "What were your plans for our alliance?"

"Well, peace amongst the two peoples, assistance to one if the other were to ever need it. Why do you ask as if there are other motives?"

Islix sighed, looking to the worn shield on the wall beside him. "Do you think I am idiot enough to believe that?"

"It is the truth! Whatever do you mean?"

"*Ozburn*." Islix emphasized. "There was no alliance. You never wanted such a thing to exist, but what you did want was a chance to overpower the Indomnis. To overthrow me, from within my own walls." He said quietly, as if to avoid being overheard.

Ozburn didn't speak up for a bit, losing himself in thought. But the silence alone was the biggest admission of guilt.

"How?" Ozburn whispered, the only word he could muster while actively avoiding the eyeline of the Indomnis general.

"Your treatment of others was enough of a tell that you had other goals. If you cannot treat your own people right, you certainly would not start with strangers." Islix thought of the bruising and scars along Zinnia's wrists, the shadows beneath Camellia's eyes, and the skittish nature of Lillian. There would be more evidence if he was given the chance to look even further into the matter, he was sure of it.

"Are you going to give them back or not?" Ozburn asked, cracking the stoic nature of Islix in that single question.

"They are people, Ozburn." Islix spoke up once more.

"They are my workers!" He shot up from his chair.

"Not anymore." Zinnia allowed herself into the room with the two leaders, carefully shutting the door behind her.

Ozburn's eyes widened, taking in all of Zinnia from head to toe as she made her way to Islix's side. She made sure to look the Royan general in the eyes, maintaining her fearless stance. Her shoulders straight and her hands clasped together, Islix cursed within himself, wondering what her presence would do to Ozburn. Her clothing stood out the most, with the Indomnis black and red colors carefully fitted across her body.

"What are you doing here, Zinnia? I told you to stay away from here." Islix's low voice pointed sharply in her direction. She met his sharp gaze with her gentle smile, the one she reserved only for Islix.

"I know you want to speak for us, to keep me safe. But a part of me wanted to say it myself. To tell Ozburn he no longer owns any of us." Zinnia's smile dropped to a softened glare at the general across from them. Islix looked surprised for a brief moment before returning to Ozburn's increasingly annoyed glower, an arm protectively extending around Zinnia.

"I want to thank you for everything you did for me. Everything," Zinnia pulled up her sleeves, letting her arms show off the faded bruises and scars, still painted with a mixture of red and purple. "I know I'm not the only one, the first one you have done things like this to. But now, I get to be the last one. My body is no longer your punching bag. None of us are." She looked from her arms to Ozburn. "You're a disgrace for a leader." She said, making sure every word came out with emphasis. Islix's hand settled on her lower back, as if to lend some form of strength in his silence, watching Ozburn's face redden with frustration.

"Then so be it. Stay with these beasts for all I care. But do not ever think of coming back, do you hear me?" Ozburn said with finality. "Be whatever whore you choose to be, Zinnia."

"Understood. So long as you do not come back here either." She said with a soft tone and gentle bow of her head.

General Ozburn shook his head, storming out of the room from the door behind Islix and Zinnia, the slam echoing around them.

XIV

When Islix confirmed with a few soldiers that General Ozburn had left the Indomnis castle for good, he sighed with relief, giving his thanks to the soldiers who took watch at the front of the castle for their patience. He then requested them to tell Aslin and the others of the situation, stating he would discuss further plans once the dust settled and everyone had a chance to calm down from the intensity of the day.

Islix closed the door to the meeting room, looking at Zinnia's uncertain expression.

Now that they were alone again, he had to do something he hated, and reprimand her for sneaking away from Aslin.

He stared at her with such an intense gaze, her face dropped, her honey eyes looking to the stone floor. She braced herself, barely ready for whatever was to come next.

"I-I know I shouldn't have interrupted, but—"

"But what? Ozburn is unstable, what possible reason could you have for going against direct orders? Going against the one thing I had asked of you?"

Islix's voice grew increasingly frustrated, his arms crossing over his chest.

Zinnia pouted, unsure how to express what had gone through her head when she snuck away from Aslin's apparently-not-careful-enough eyes.

"Well?" He asked, demanding an answer.

"I was worried about you and I didn't want to leave you alone with him." Zinnia responded in a soft voice, her flushed face apologetic.

"Zinnia, I am twice his size!" Islix scolded. He placed a thoughtful hand over his mouth, unsure how to proceed from here. She braved her fear to make sure he was safe.

Regardless of how much he towered over any of the Royan, Zinnia still snuck off to check in on him.

And barged in to protect him from Ozburn.

The thought was more amusing than anything else, leaving him laughing to himself.

"Did you think I could not handle him if he decided to turn on me?"

"Not at all. You went so much out of your way to help us when we needed it, I wanted to do the same. You don't deserve getting in trouble for helping me, for helping us." She added.

"Zinnia." Islix sat down on the meeting table, giving her his previous seat across from him. "You need to be more cautious than this. As much as I love how much you care, I asked you to stay away from here for a reason." His voice softened as he reached over, taking her small face into his oversized hand.

"I guess you can see I don't take orders very well." Zinnia giggled, prompting a choked back laugh from Islix.

"I suppose so." He leaned close, running his thumb over her warm cheek. Her stare came with a softened expression, one reminiscent of when they met. "While I adore that about you, and how much you care about others, please do not ever put yourself at risk for me, or anyone, again."

"And what if I cannot promise that?" She retorted, drawing him closer with every passing breath.

"Who knows, my dear." Islix kept her still, brushing his lips against hers. "Consequences must come for your actions." He said in a low voice before kissing her softly, feeling her hand thread through his own. In what should have been a short instance, Islix felt no hesitation from Zinnia to stop him, licking the entrance of her lips in a need surpassing the night prior.

"I could not fathom losing you, Zinnia." Islix pulled her up into his arms, placing her against the wall. Her legs wrapped around his waist, feeling him press her harder against the cold stone. His lips desperately overcame hers, the gap between them closing up. Islix held Zinnia up against the wall, ready to give up breathing just to keep tasting her. Wedged between her thighs, he used his weight to keep her steady, pressing further against her when he began to feel warmth grow between them. His arms wrapped around her lower back, his hands dipping below the hem of her skirt, feeling her skin rest in his palms.

Zinnia's hands settled around his neck, one sliding down his chest. She pulled away the straps to his leather armor, letting herself feel his skin against her fingertips. She felt the subtle groan rumble in his throat, leaving her wanting to explore every part of him she could get her hands on.

The soft mend of his lips against hers drew affectionately with all the patience in the world for her, working against his own desires. He didn't allow his grip on her to loosen even for a moment. He pulled part of her skirt down, her warm skin reveling in the cold air. In turn, she pulled away the straps from his shoulders, lowering them before Islix pulled away and placed his face in her collarbone.

"I cannot bear the idea of being apart from you." Islix pressed his lips into her neck, biting down into her soft skin. The soft moan leaving her mouth almost

had him bite her all the way through. His pants
tightened at the sound, ready to take her as he did the
night before. His blood pumped hard through his
veins, yearning to lay claim on her. His need was
increasing, alongside his rough heartbeat.

Zinnia struggled to steady her racing thoughts, her
hands tracing up from his hair to the base of his horns.
Her lingering touch made him feel as good as it did in
her room. He fumbled to remove his clothes, his
hands tearing off the straps from his armor, reaching
for the belt of his pants while he kept Zinnia steady
against the wall. He made quick work of her blouse,
and soon, the two had bare themselves to one another.
He backed away, his hands holding her still as his eyes
ran over every inch of her body.

Islix felt her soft hands run over both horns, leaving
him running on only instincts. The once soft rumble
of his throat became a feral growl, like that of a wild
animal hunting its prey. He found her neck once more
and bit down, harder than he had ever before, drawing
a small stream of blood into his mouth. Her blood was
unlike anything he ever tasted, leaving Islix no more a
man than his impulses.

His hands cupped her ass, holding her in place as
he pressed his cock into her, swears slipping from
under his breath while he let the feeling of her warmth

overtake him. The light thrust of her hips had him pushing into her as far as he could get, ripping himself from her neck to take her lips once more.

With every feral move into her, a moan left her. She pressed her bare breasts against him leaving him sensitive, quickening every push into her before the most delirious noise left her lips, the shudder of her body and her scratching at his back felt as if she were begging him to go deeper into her. Each mewl spilling from her lips left him just as needy, leaving him pounding into her as hard as he could into the wall, finishing himself off inside of her. He pumped every part of himself into her until he could no longer bear the act.

Islix remained breathless, the air around them matching the heat lingering on their skin. He kissed down the side of her face, a content but heavy sigh leaving him. Zinnia remained still, clutching onto him for life, his warmth drawing her into his chest. She laid her head against him, closing her eyes as she tried to catch her breath. A lighthearted rumble in his throat followed with his arms wrapped protectively around her back. Her hand slid up to his hair, playfully letting the strands run through her fingertips.

"I have a selfish request of you, Zinnia." Islix settled into his embrace around her, letting the quick tune of her heart guide his next words. "Stay here with me. You and the others should live in the castle. There is more than enough space."

"Islix, I worry about such a choice."

"Zinnia." He pleaded, hands tightening around her. She leaned in close, settling further into him.

"I will think about it, Islix. But what if you grow tired of me?"

"I could never. You have my heart in your hands." He breathed, leaving a kiss to her forehead. "Stay with me, Zinnia." His voice lowered, pulling back to look at her. His black eyes settled on her with a saddened expression, their starry sparkle now melancholy. She thought carefully before speaking again.

"If I stay, what does that mean for you?"

"Everything." He smiled, perking back up at the question. "I will spend every day doing whatever it takes to keep you happy here. Anything and everything."

Zinnia shifted her adoring smile into a thoughtful one. Seconds turned into minutes, and Islix grew nervous as he watched her. He wanted her around, just as he did in the Royan castle. Whether their dire circumstances had occurred or not, Islix felt he would have still ended up here, begging for Zinnia to stay with him.

"Would you miss me if I left?" Her question a bare whisper between them.

"With all my heart." Islix kept his eyes on her, hoping with everything.

"I would miss you, too." She pressed her forehead against his, feeling his arms tighten around her, a heavy sigh of relief leaving his chest. He pulled up her face, eagerly stealing her lips once more.

Islix refused to let her go, the two remaining in the meeting room for much of the day.

XV

Three months came and went in the Indomnis castle, with each day as uneventful as the last. Within this time, Zinnia, Camellia, and Lillian found themselves barely adjusting, going from their daily duties to the Royan castle to such quiet days in the Indomnis kingdom. While the three women decided to take up their time in different ways, all agreed the peace was needed, letting every day away from the Royan kingdom bring some semblance of consistency to their lives.

Zinnia took it upon herself to take each day easy, relishing in the newfound freedom, and learning more about what she wanted, from both herself and from the new life she had a chance to build. As soon as each day began, she quickly let archery practice among the gardens become her newest obsession. In the night hours, Islix would seldom spend his evenings doing anything else, keeping Zinnia at his side all throughout the days and nights.

Her bravery in speaking out against General Ozburn and her tendency to overhear everything that had occurred in the Royan castle during her time as a maid earned her a place beside Islix, as both a partner and someone with knowledge of the Royan kingdom who plotted against the Indomnis, among other kingdoms throughout her time working for them.

There was more than enough work to be done in dealing with the Royan kingdom and their general, but Islix could only bide their time, until Ozburn would try something else.

Lillian would find herself immersed in books, every day a new adventure, so long as the book in her hands would hold her attention. She could be easily found lounging among the flowers, with her head in the pages of her latest book. Much of her days she spent reclusive, keeping her distance from everyone by taking up her daytime residence in either the Indomnis library or within the span of the gardens. The better parts of her days were when she had been left alone, with minimal interactions, except for Zinnia and Camellia's daily check ins.

All she needed was her peace and quiet. From there, she could read and let the day pass her by, unbothered and free from responsibility.

Because if Lillian did anything to disturb her new routine, she was unsure if she could handle the consequences, the flood of thoughts that would accompany the silence. Until she was ready to process everything that had happened in the last few years of her life, Lillian would bide her time in the Indomnis castle as she did in the Royan castle; by reading everything and anything she could get her hands on, until the books ran out.

For almost everyone living in the castle, life had a sense of stability for the most part.

But for one, a small feeling of foreboding took up the air around her.

In the mere moments of peace, the clash of metal echoed in the sparring hall. Camellia made it a point to join Zinnia in the art of self defense, taking up a short sword, and fighting as her extracurricular. Unlike the others, she let her hobby take up far more of her time, sparring and clashing with whoever was around. Even with Aslin's prying eyes, Camellia would take any chance she could get to hold a sword in her hand and practice.

On her better days, Camellia would be found challenging other Indomnis soldiers of lower ranks, helping them to correct their postures and stances in the process. She was hands on, her standoffish persona dissolving in the face of these small clashes. Camellia took a sense of responsibility for those new to battle, never pushing them beyond their limits, but encouraging many to practice and ways to improve themselves.

But when it came to those of higher ranks, she would only do her best, and keep her guard high. It wasn't long before word ran through the castle of a once maid now training Indomnis soldiers.

Aslin of the Indomnis, second in command to General Islix, and leader of the Indomnis guard, did not take very well to this.

To Be Continued!

Thank you for picking up my latest project! The entire concept came as a surprise to me, but I humbly decided to run with it!

In our next book, softly titled *Of Indomitable Courage*, we take the time to see everything from the perspective of Aslin, second in command to General Islix, and leader of the guard. I'm very excited for the sequel to come, to show everyone just who Aslin of the Indomnis is!

See you all soon!

~Nik

www.ingramcontent.com/pod-product-compliance
Lightning Source LLC
Chambersburg PA
CBHW031518010826

48973CB00013B/2687